THE OTHER GUY™

Cyrus Williams

This novel is a work of fiction. Comedically so. Any reference to real events, businesses, organizations and locales are intended only to give this fiction a sense of reality and authenticity. Any resemblance to actual persons, living or dead, is entirely and pitifully coincidental.

ISBN-10: 0990311619
ISBN-13: 978-0990311614

DEDICATION

This book is dedicated to the youth. Whether of age, heart or soul, they are our tomorrow. You are our tomorrow.

To my incredible wife – Erika – I love you. To my children – Cyrus, Madde and Sydni – you are the future I never knew would be so wonderful. To my brothers and sisters – Carl, Larry, Ron, Terry, Paula, Luanna and Andrea – this work culminates your support and our experiences. Thankfully, you all, unknowingly, signed release forms.

Most importantly, I send the greatest dedication and gratitude to three individuals. No proper notation for their contributions exists. They are the true originators of the smiles this writer ever generated. To my dearly departed parents – Clarence and Bertha Williams – and to the Almighty God... without all three, I could not be me.

All my love and then some,
Cy.

INGREDIENTS

Artificial imitation pages, words [which may contain one of more of the following: humor, misuse of the English language, exaggerations, reflective thought], punctuation, numbers, publishing [used as a preservative].

FOREWORD

If you are looking for an entertaining take on life, keep reading!

If you are looking for a book with a plot – a significant, hard plot – stop reading, make sure this book is paid for, then give it to someone else.

Seriously, how often does *your* life reflect a perfectly orchestrated novel? How often have you said, "This is not my day [my week, my year, my lifespan]?"

I understand without really understanding, primarily because prior to writing this book, I realized I knew nothing... period! Now that I understand more about things and about myself, I know I know nothing... question mark!

So, if splashing around in this writer's psyche sounds enticing, bring a life preserver and a pooper-scooper, cuz whatever ain't liquid enough to wade through, pick it up and dispose of it properly.

Nonetheless, go with the flow. Eventually, your trying times will end and I might stop laughing at you for believing it would.

Remember, to everybody else, you are The Other Guy.

ACKNOWLEDGEMENTS

cover art by Blake Kandzer
Kandzer.com

cover design by Cyrus Williams

photography by Cyrus O. Williams

Also...

like The Other Guy at
facebook.com/TheOtherGuyBook

hate him in 140 characters or less at
twitter.com/TheOtherGuyBook

or do whatever at
instagram.com/TheOtherGuyBook

and for some reason...
pinterest.com/TheOtherGuyBook

to stay abreast of Cyrus news and upcoming events, please visit
CyrusWilliams.com

oh yeah, annnd...
#MyTruckCheated

FIRST CHAPTER

The scene, an alley at night. An alley like any alley found in a growing city. Dark, cold, hollow.

An alley you would walk into just to see if a wino or a junkie is curled up next to an unforgiving brick wall. An alley you would walk into... if you had the guts.

A street lamp shines above, shedding more light on your fears than the alley below. In the distance, you hear water slowly dripping from a faucet you cannot see.

Did you hear that? Was it a door or a large rat? And what was that? Footsteps? Faint footsteps?

Maybe.

Whatever the sounds, they build.

Is someone there? Anyone?

Yeah. Right. Surely, no one is dumb enough to hang out in that alley. Surely? Right?

Something emerges from the darkness. Something big has moved into that one section the street lamp contemplates illuminating. No, not something, SOMEONE lurks in the alley!

You discern its silhouette. Your fear grows.

Running very fast seems like a really, really smart thing to do, but fascination with the unknown cements your body where you stand. The silhouette comes closer, getting bigger. And now of all times you choose to actually have a conversation with yourself:

"Run."

"No."

"It's coming closer. At least walk."

"No!"

"The coroner won't list our cause of death as 'Fascination with the Unknown.'"

"So...?"

"Run, dammit!"

Eventually, you win the argument with yourself and stay. The silhouette advances and then you hear it. A booming, deep voice. Not deep enough to sing for the Temptations, but very, very deep.

"I am Dinky."

Deep and forever approaching.

"At 220 pounds, I resemble mean. I do not look nice. I do not act nice. I am not nice!"

His silhouette draws closer.

"A big man who finds pleasure inflicting pain, witnessing anyone suffer amuses me more than prime-time television ever dreams to. Personally awarding someone punishment dispenses complete satisfaction throughout and within."

His silhouette gives way to the street lamp and he *is* big! A black man barely in his twenties, wearing a dark grey suit, whiter-than-white shirt, a mauve, black and green tie and... black Reebok tennis shoes?

His face rings familiarity. Years of familiarity. And his name? Dinky??? Who would forget that?

His friendly face betrays his soliloquy, but his size...?

Whoa!

Retreating from the alley while keeping an eye on Dinky, you notice a little redhead girl licking an all-evening sucker standing nearby.

Go ahead, tell her to run in case Dinky actually shares thought patterns with gun-packing postal workers. But nooo, you just haaaaaaave to learn the truth. Will "Alley Man" in the suit and tennis shoes hurt that girl?

Dinky walks and talks.

"I hate happiness and everything associated with it. Bright colors, summer love and smiling little kids missing their front teeth."

Exiting the alley, he notices the redhead girl.

"Yeah, I hate little kids," he growls.

This act captures the girl's attention. She smiles, revealing no front teeth. She offers Dinky a lick of her sucker. He slaps it out of her hand and growls again. Stunned, the girl looks at her raised hand which held a sucker mere moments ago. Tears gather in her eyes and her little hand becomes a little fist. Dinky, apparently happy with what he had done, leans over, putting his face in front hers.

"Yeah, I hate little kids. And I hope my breath stinks."

It does.

Her eyes reluctantly faucet tears that drag race down her face. She again stares at her raised fist and trembles.

"Are you scared little girl?" he growls thrice. "You sh—"

Dinky never finishes his sentence. The little redhead girl shuffles his jaw, knocking him out with one punch.

The scene, the same alley, four hours later.

Dinky has nary a clue about his present location or situation. Sudden unconsciousness can do that to a person. As the sandman withdraws his hammer from Dinky's head, our so-called hero believes his bed lies under him and his alarm clock beeps. Soon, the truth won't set him free.

"What a dream," Dinky belches as he blindly reaches for the snooze button. "Please, just another five minutes."

His attempts at turning his alarm off fail. And the beeps get louder. And louder. And then, the beeps stop.

"Finally," he sighs. "But... were those air brakes? Do I really want to see... NOOOOOOOO!!!"

Garbage!

Unless you possess a warped appreciation pertaining to offal, it sucks. It sucks big time if this offal deposits itself on your whiter-than-white shirt with you in it.

Last night while Dinky harassed a cute little girl, sanitation engineers went on strike. Also unbeknownst to our hero, he forcibly reclined in the one alley the garbage people decided to empty their trucks into when they went on strike. Eventually, someone must remove the offal, but for now, Dinky understands why some soiled diapers hold their contents better than others.

"Author!"

Is that Dinky screaming? What the heck could he be whining for now?

"Author," he thunders, "I know you can read me. Listen: you think this book is fiction, although everything typed actually happens to me. One man's fiction non-fictions another man and your fiction hurts me! Since this book catalogs my life, let me write it, let me think it, let me live it. Dammit, let me control my own life!"

Author reflects on Dinky's testimony. Who knows? His way may sell more books... or land a movie contract.

Hmmmmmmmmmmmm.

"Thank you," Dinky replies, er, I reply.

Now that this book breathes my breath, wallowing in this garbage delays our introductions. We can commence while we walk to my house.

Ummm, this might take a while. Can I catch up with you on the next page?

There. Hey! Why are you running? Oh, the smell bothers you? Or the sight? Or the people pointing at us?

Puh-leeze. Hold your nose, close your eyes and read.

Do you remember the line, "that always happens to the other guy?" Well, I wear his shoes.

My real name is Richard Deankey.

Yes, Deankey.

My parents believed they should maintain their own identities – and names – even after their marriage, scheduled for next year. According to them, "our children will bask in the radiance from our physical and emotional union." So, my father, Oscar Dean, and my mother, Kath E Key, named their three offspring Deankey.

Despite their genes, I possess handsome qualities. 5'11", 220 athletic pounds, been around 22 years and I dress well. Despite all of the above, I... uh... never mind.

Intelligence acquaints me. It acquaints my baby sis more. Something for further discussions. Over cocktails, maybe?

Ahem. Few other positive attributes can accompany me, due to "The Other Guy" complex. The rest of this chapter proves my point.

AT HOME.

Fingernails scraping a chalkboard. Nice feeling? Cool sound? Think you could live with it as someone's voice? Well, every time I arrive at my front door, it comes. Without fail.

My father! Pops!

Whenever Pops starts yelling for whatever, the women-folk cater. I avoid him as much as possible, which is relatively easy. He rarely leaves his den. In fact, he vacates his den so infrequently that if the dude has a job, he hides the fact from me.

We seldom confront each other. He likes the arrangement. I love it, primarily because I hate his voice. It peels my tooth enamel.

His voice? It once maintained a magnificent quantity of testosterone before the accident about eight years ago.

He played defensive line for the semi-pro football team. After practice, he usually hitchhiked downtown. On one excursion, he probed an attractive, young lady strolling past him, saran-wrapped in a candy apple red, tight, tight, tight mini-dress and sporting six-inch heels.

Pops floated on her like a toxic gas cloud. When they walked over a ventilation grate, she tripped and he fell on her, lodging a spiked heel in his groin. The spike embedded in him so deeply that when the woman saw her shoe in his lap, she thought the heel broke off and dropped down the grate.

Come to think of it, Pops shared numerous stories like that. I wonder if "The Other Guy" travels hereditarily.

Anyway, despite the accident, Pops owns a massive collection of rock hard muscles, enough for me to literally hide behind him. His size seriously inhibits teasing from normal people. Moronic individuals tease him once and incur large hospital bills as mementos. Moron and forgetfulness condiment my personality.

As previously mentioned, every time I come home, he starts yelling. At least once a month, my temper erupts. Also, as mentioned, my sister and/or Mom serve him. But one day, one frightful day, they went shopping, leaving us alone in the house. I was relaxing in my room upstairs and he lingered in his den, as usual. But then he did it. He just had to break the peace, badgering me to get him something.

"Ignore him," echoed repeatedly in my skull. "Ignore him."

I wish I did. Good golly, I wish I did.

Whenever he opened/opens/will open his mouth, his voice taxies me closer to the edge of sanity. No different than on that day. And on that day, my id inevitably blundered.

"Get off your lazy carcass," I barked, "fetch your own tofu and sell that voice to Mattel for their next line of talking dolls."

Big, big, big, big, big mistake!

First, dead silence. I soon recognized some hurried, heavy, hard footsteps. They got real loud and stopped real close. My door then exploded and there he stood. The top of the doorway hid his eyebrows, but I knew they were in the pissed-off position.

Summoning every bit of pride available, I walked up to him and said in my toughest male-dominant voice...

"Tofu?"

Too late! He reached down, grabbed my face and picked me up. Sight, breathing and speech were effectively eliminated. All that and my feet dangled. Then all of the sudden, I had the power of flight, the ability to crash through walls and sufficient inertia to leave my impression on the ground.

Looking high at that new exit point from the house, I understood sufficient velocity on an object will let said object leave a cartoon-like outline on the obstacle it traveled through. As a matter of fact, the hole in the wall looks just like the hole in the ground, a la Wile E. Coyote.

Hey, I tried avoiding the wall, but Pops' father-aided lateral velocity exceeded my forward drive. In other words, HE THREW ME!!!

Pops later ordered a special window for the hole, reminding me that his tofu commands my attention if he so desires.

My mother! Kath E Key!

Her full first name is Kath and no period follows the E, her full middle name. Punctuation would make it stand for something.

I love the woman, but her presence yearns me like sharing Pops' companionship. Her beauty lies somewhere. Just not on her.

Cute? Possibly. Personable? At times. Motherly? Get real!

Birth remains the most gripping memory Mom supplies. I remember the doctor holding me by the ankles, whispering, "I'm praying for you."

Mom and moi usually cross paths in the kitchen. When hunger hauls me there, she shows up. My taste buds rarely crave food at home, though. Reasons forthcoming.

One reason open for discussion now: Mom cannot cook! On those oh-so-seldom episodes she processes food, people die. She means well, but Mom cannot prepare a menu without someone contracting food poisoning.

One more thing about the mum patriarch, despite her petite size and panda bear deportment, if provoked, everyone leaves the house. No matter who or what volcanoed her, whoever dawdles after her initial eruption gets a projectile skipped off their head. Pops says her accuracy surpasses that of any quarterback he broke. And he should know. Mom ricocheted her favorite throwing instrument – a skillet – off his head a time or two.

My sister. Swydni!
Stupid name, brilliant person, tough attitude. Perfect example: Pops often called Swydni from her laboratory to fetch his remote control whenever it was more than an arm's length away. She hated this with a passion. On one occasion, he requested her repeatedly and she had had enough. Swydni concocted a wafer-thin universal remote about the size of a credit card and slapped it on the back of Pops' hand. She said bio-electrical current powers the thing, in addition to affixing it to his hand. All this plus a lifetime guarantee. Swydni told Pops his death will definitely precede the remote's.

FRIENDS.
Russell!
Actually, I only have one friend. And he has no first name. Just... Russell. Hmmm.

Anyway, Russell and I first met eight years ago. He and his mother moved into the house next door during the worst winter on record. Because Russell never talked much then, Mrs. Russell believed he would not make a lot of friends; ergo, she bought him a very big puppy for companionship.

During this time of year, a lot of teenagers get their drivers license. When the boys in the neighborhood get theirs, they drive recklessly around the block in the snow. Doughnuts and such. My first encounter with Russell occurred completing my yearly ritual for these newly christened drivers.

I make a snowman in my backyard and thoroughly water it down. After setting out overnight, it becomes solid ice. Packing a layer of snow over the iceman gives it a snowman appearance. Placing it in someone's yard near the street, the action waits for a witless kid's destructive tendencies with a motor vehicle. To date, car damages total appoximately $175,004.11.

This particular year, I tried placing the snowman in Russell's front yard. The Man on High, with his insanely creative sense of humor, used this opportunity for my specially scheduled meeting with... the dog!

While carrying my current model of destruction next door, bombastic claps fractured the air the instant I invaded Russell landscape. Cascading

>>tha-BOOMs<< fringed on the edge of solid sound. Could it have been lightning? Should it have been lightning?

Anyway, the sounds of thunder and a stampede registered major dB. Turning towards the source, a train with fur rushed upon me and parked on my chest. The dog had tackled and pinned me with a paw on each shoulder and commenced eating my iceman which landed right next to my head. While I lay there, bombarded with shredded ice and saliva, a midget wearing a turban approached, strapped a saddle on the dog, climbed on top of it and rode it into a garage. Shortly thereafter, the midget returned with a towel and brass knuckles. He handed me the towel, put on the knuckles, introduced himself very politely, asked if I would be his friend and knocked me out with one punch.

Of course the midget in the turban was Russell. Thinking back, he never committed another harmful act at my expense.

Presumably.

When we first met, he acquired his social etiquette from Bugs Bunny and Foghorn Leghorn. Ya' know wut I mean, son?

Although, Russell maintains his shortcomings – 5'4" – his attitude makes him one of the best people in town. He seldom talks and he has an offbeat mystique that just seems extra odd for someone his size. Beyond wit, Russell usually contributes positively toward any conversation, making people approach circumstances with different perspectives.

Quote: Opinions are absorbed faster if served on humor.

Russell personifies this. Anyone he offends simply exhibits insecurity about the situation or themselves. If I do something where he would believe it is wrong, I habitually cannot do it. Russell enhances me this way. Even if he cannot unearth what I devise, what Russell might think stops me every time.

I want to and try to be good people. I just slip up every once in a while. Russell never does and he keeps me on my toes. His entire make-up guarantees him a place behind the Pearly Gates when he expires, unless he personally made reservations elsewhere.

Every so often I learn something new about him. I question if I really know my best friend. Just last week, for example, I saw him enter an adult bookstore, place an order and leave. For reasons that are none of your business, I knew the woman behind the counter. I walked in afterwards and asked her about her last customer. From what I understand, Russell knows the attendant much better than I ever will. Despite my intense interrogations, she would not crack.

Actually, I begged. She still said nothing.

Multiple situations like this fuel peculiar suspensions toward Russell. With all of my heart and soul, I know at least half the populace of Carlisle practice their inevitable network television interview:

"I just can't believe it. Russell is the nicest person who ever lived. Besides, I never imagined those infomercial knives could do all that to a person."

Oh! And women?! THEY LOVE HIM!!! I hate it, but they love him. I really hate it and they really love him! Hard!

No proof ever came my way regarding Russell doing the nasty. The way women talk to him, though, he could get more butt than the only ashtray at a smokers' convention.

Mrs. Russell!

This woman hates me! Who could blame her? She has had to replace six doors, quite possibly because of me.

No... seven. I forgot yesterday.

And not seven different doors anywhere throughout the house, mind you. Instead, the front door, seven times. No matter how thick, how strong or how durable, they do not stop me. Through no fault of my own, the dog chases me out of the house. If I stop to open the door, the dog enjoys my ham.

Unlike my parents, Mrs. Russell never speaks to me. I prefer it that way, because she reeks from chewing tobacco. Not the normal stuff either, she puts a cigar between her cheek and gums.

The dog! Apocalypse!

This fur mountain of a Great Dane must be a mutant. And it truly cherishes an exclusive snack.

Me.

I again admit, "moron" and "forgetful" signs drape around my neck. If Russell leaves me unaccompanied anywhere in his house, Apocalypse thinks fast food. The mutt looks at me like my underwear contains bacon bits. Apocalypse TREATS me like my underwear contains bacon bits!

Okay, okay, enough backstory. Besides, my house lies right over there.

Scan those construction workers installing that front door. Russell lives there. If you read closely, you can see the ugly one with the five o'clock shadow.

You got it! Mrs. Russell!

How long are you staying with me? The whole book? Well, an ordinary week in my life probably unveils. It undoubtedly duplicates what you stomached already, only worse.

You did check out the cop car following us, right? She usually bothers me if I am companion-less. Hopefully – HOPEFULLY – introductions need not transpire.

We better go in. Before it rains.

SUBLIMINAL CHAPTER

Ahem, please remember to leave a review for my book/life somewhere – social media, fave retailer, post-it note on somebody's forehead.

And did you read the Foreword?

Okay, go on to the next chapter.

NEXT CHAPTER

9am? The last time I hit the doorstep this late, Officer Hazel nearly nabbed me.

As the front door creaks open, the expected sign in the foyer disappoints me not: "If you want to stay, you have to pay. $5 at the door, ten bucks and your buttocks if forced."

One time, I dared Mom and Pops to take the daily rent. Never underestimate the strength of a woman.

Walking past the collection bucket, my room beckons while... huh? Was that...?

Oh, my teeth!

Resembling a high-powered laser beam with a singular, destructive purpose, it searches around and through walls, zeroing in on yours truly. From the dark, dank corner of the den, each microsecond of travel time increases the intensity geometrically. When it hits, it hurts. Pops' voice!

"Boy!"

I scream. No choice. He drew blood.

"Shut up and come here," he squawks.

I wipe the blood from my ears, answering his summons. For the first time in quite some time, we will occupy the same room. Big thrill.

Hesitantly, I approach his basement sanctuary. Reaching for the doorknob, the familiar sensation re-tingles my teeth.

"Stay out there," he squeaks. "No need to see you to talk to you."

Thankyou, thankyou, thankyou!

"Today's your mother's birthday."

More blood.

"Get her something nice if you plan on staying here. You paying attention, boy?"

I should pay attention, but repressing the voice-induced contortions requires complete concentration and... my teeth? They feel fine! Did he shut up? Better say the customary...

"Yeah, Pops."

"You better do something this year. Every year you walk in yur mother's surprise party empty handed, spouting some mess 'bout her

11

birthday being last year. It's *my* job to forget the day that makes her iron less so it offsets the wrinkles Father Time gives her. It's yur mother's day, boy. Get 'er something!"

"Whatever you say, Pops."

Another customary reply. He already exceeded the father/son conversational time limit. If he keeps quiet a few more seconds, my tush ventures elsewhere.

One Mississippi, two Missi–

"One more thing, boy."

Puh-leeze!

"What's that smell?

Whoops. Forgot the diaper on my shoulder.

"Your mother's not in the kitchen, is she?" he interjects while slapping the back of his hand. Must be changing channels.

"Tell her we're eating out."

Hot diggity. Meals O'Happy for everybody. Just once I wish the unreasonable facsimile of yesteryear suffering throughout this here habitat returned.

Alas, Pops did finally pipe down. Might as well linger another four Mississippies, making sure he wants nothing else.

Voyaging up and away from hell-den, I remember you [the reader] have never "seen" my house before. If you have some time, would you mind a tour? Well then, vamanos.

First, imagine what Pops' den looks like. Picture an eerie, cold, vampiric sports bar, complete with his former team's taxadermied mascot, Tempie the Turtle.

The house has central air conditioning, but Pops wanted a portable a/c, too. The television supplies the only illumination in there. That and the many neon memorabilia from his semi-pro football days. The doctors told him he could regain his blitzing prowlness. Medically speaking, he was, and still is, in excellent condition. Psychologically speaking... well, one can say the heel encounter took away some of his manhood.

Ouch.

When we take a left at the top of the stairs, like thus, witness the family room, which the family rarely uses. It is a healthy-sized room, as are most of the rooms here. About twenty-two... twenty-three feet directly in front of us rests the master bedroom. Come on.

I said, come on!

The family seldom utilizes the family room, because Mom and Pops, when together, routinely stayed in the master bedroom area and the pandemonium they make keeps Sis and me away. Opening the door slowly, you view... yes! The mattresses covered in their original plastic packaging.

What? Why dreary yellow plastic? Because they bought the mattresses when they bought the house! Over 20 years ago!

Oooooh, the mysteries this house haveth.

Answering question number one: Pops sleeps in the den and Mom sleeps... Mom sleeps... Mom sleeps somewhere. I never thought about it before. Where does Mom sleep? Does Mom sleep?

Who cares?

Answering question number two: do they get busy? Does mummy and poppa embrace on the plain of total sexuality?

Yyyep!!! Generating more noise pollution than mating moose do when they do the do!

Behind that door to the right, the source resides. Behind it abides... the master bath.

Parents engaging in physical fondness repulse most children, if they ever do give their Mom and Pops the benefit of transpiring in such an activity. Whenever I spend more than six hours at home, including sleep, not hearing my birthers "enjoy" themselves shocks me. The master bath – or more precisely, the hot tub – frequently yields its glossy finish to unbridled satisfaction performed by bumping baby boomers.

All those years of liquid love.

The whole neighborhood recognized it, too. In fact, the bedlam split the neighbors into two factions: the women, who tried to get their portly husbands to act more like Pops, and the men, who tried to get away from their wives long enough to turn Pops in for disturbing the peace.

Strange as it sounds, water aphrodisiacs my father. It also quenches the effects of his "accident." Whenever he hears or feels water and Mom is nowhere around, domestic animals get nervous. Unhygenically speaking, water indubitably entices Pops' reproductive wants.

I tested this theory's validity once, being the type of son who cherishes his father. Mom had guests over and Pops, in the den, slumbered within the crosshairs of my double-pump, water balloon shotgun. Hiding behind the life size wax statue of him in uniform, two perfect blasts shot forth, plummeting his mustache. He revived, not mad, but excited.

Very excited!

After shooting a glance at a scared Tempie, he sprinted upstairs toward his unsuspecting comrade. I faintly heard Mom say, "Oscar, honey. Have you met...?"

His hormones overwhelmed her introductions as he carried her to the tub and... noise. Soon followed by... sirens. This time, a chubby hubby escaped his undersexed wife.

Weird, huh?

These activities diminished a touch after Mom personally situated whisper-silent toilets throughout the house last year. But, uh, she maintains the temperature and water levels in the hot tub.

Come. The tour continues.

Leaving the master suite, tarry left through the family room toward the stairs. No, we can go up in a minute. Keep going, yeah, into the living room. Into the museum.

What can I say, other than my parents are weird?

Weird. I use that word often. Go figure.

The lighting arrangement in this room shows how Oscar and Kath E cannot appreciate their children's accomplishments as normal parents can. The north side reflects their adoration of my grade school achievements.

Whenever I brought home a finger painting, Pops bought a frame for it and Mom bought a refrigerator to hang it on. The south side shows their munificence of Swydni's grade school projects. Whenever she won the county expo's science fair, Mom bought a pedestal for her project and Pops bought a spotlight. Most of Swydni's early plastic compositions melted.

My older brother, Rhys, did very-little-to-nothing in school. Whatever acknowledgment for anything he accomplished, he took with him for no other reason than being the jerk he is.

Last I heard, he uses his trophies for antennas. He also hangs his plaques backwards with the face against the wall.

Jerk!

Anyway, as we bank left, look right. The breezeway, garage and Pops' weight room are back there. Again, to my knowledge, he seldom leaves his den, except to... you know. But he evidently gets in the weight room. How else can he stay massively rugged? Just some things to ponder, in case of a sequel. Keep walking.

Next, the kitchen. Whenever you find yourself in this danger zone, stay on guard. Mom may have something incubating.

Notice the ceiling and upper 1/3 of all the walls. One night, Swydni induced a friend over for dinner. Mom whipped up a soup, I think, and had it simmering while everyone conjured in the dining room. Pops – out of his den and in a rarer jovial mood – was telling us about one of his football "concussion parties" when an explosion interrupted him.

Mom's entree left the pot.

You can tell it must have spewed up and spread out like liquid hitting the floor. Of course, this turquoise blotch directly above the island range marks where the soup first crashed after vaporizing the range hood. The psychedelic concentric color changes highlight the different stages where the soup unfolded outward onto the ceiling, eventually fading as it reached the walls.

When the smoke cleared and the toxic levels depreciated, Swydni's friend nearly cried with gaiety. An interior designer by trade, this "Masterpiece," as he put it, "was ta'die for."

Had it stayed in the pot, he would have.

Another example of how typically atypical this house and the occupants are broods in the refrigerator. Upon Mom's request, Pops replaced the normal light bulb with a black light. It makes the Tupperware glow like the food they contain does naturally.

No significant history concerning this breakfast bar comes hither, but if you lean on this end and look due north past the laundry room, you can visualize the back lavatory. I remember many o' times letting a Mom-cooked meal pass my lips a second time in there. It tasted better coming up, too.

Walking toward the stairs, there is something needing to be said. Before you assume my story solely consists of quip introductions and stimulating antidotes, reflect on your own history. Remember how often "this is not my day" comes into play?

Common wisdom respects everyone's uniqueness, hence comparability. The situations which shape their being... motivate their actions... predestine their permanence constitutes a particular someone's someone. Therefore, my life, being as strange as only a warped imagination can conjure, makes me no different than the person reading over your shoulder. My highway of inner spirit always has a few repair crews on it. I want to believe that someday they may finish their work.

Entropy guarantees a universal constant in lieu of the menial and catastrophic changes going on everywhere. In other words, my bad luck creates someone's good luck or vice versa. Summing up this philosophical hogwash: in the grand scheme of things, my life could be yours.

Sound bizarre? Then answer me this: does Monday come more than once a week?

We now return yon reader to the regularly scheduled program, "Quip Introductions and Stimulating Antidotes," already in progress.

Climbing these steps cues a special distinction of mine. Few people can claim walking upstairs much more often than walking down the same steps. To date, Swydni and Pops are in second and third place, respectively, for the number of times they bounced me downstairs.

Yeah, these people should occupy correctional facility space for "Dinky abuse." My family argues, though, that if their attacks were unjustified, they would inevitably parole and pain me more.

At the top, another bathroom straight ahead and a crucial decision.

Oh, puh-leeze. Get your mind out of the sewage.

The question is, should I go right, my room, or left, Swydni's room/laboratory? Right, sweet sanctuary. Left, death-defying defiance. Right, the smart move. Left, stupid.

And here lies Swydni's door! Mom and Pops never risk trespassing beyond this point. Should I constrain, too?

If you said yes, you are a fool.

Today is Swydni's "Weather Wednesday." She helps the meteorological society compile cloud-head computations. Remembering that info bears no worth. The author simply needed a convenient story to explain her absence so we can break in.

Check this out. If you knock four times...

"What?!"

Yeah, it sounds like her and yes, she personifies staunch. Keep listening.

"I'm busy. Leave a message." >>Beep<<

Is that cool or what? She modified an answering machine and hooked it up to her door. If she has a message already, it responds after two knocks.

Getting in her lab requires finesse. She detests loiterers. Swydni takes great efforts to discourage me from even thinking about unlawful entries. Thus, continuing the tour means detaching all five three-inch deadbolts, circumventing the security system and taking the surveillance camera offline.

What to do? What to do?

>>Whammm<<

Solution: Use a size 11 Reebok, attached to a size 11 foot, dodge – whoa – all projectiles, especially the lethal ones – DUCK – and appreciate having your picture taken before giving the camera the shirt off your back.

Please, step lightly and admire the hi-tech imagination of Ms. Swydni Deankey. Stay within the white lines that constitute an aisle, though. What might happen if you venture outside the passageway...? Who knows?

This room resembles a hands-on think tank in a major university. Swydni combines the desires of a withering, old mad scientist with the enthusiastic, wide-eyed amazement of a child and the stamina an Olympic athlete.

A few admiring aspects my sister keeps.

Looking throughout the room, she plainly spends time inventing, modifying and creating, while evidently remaining a girl of thirteen. Scientifically speaking, her rivals wear bifocals. Socially speaking, her rivals giggle. A rather unorthodox combination insinuating cuteness, if only she did not possess the hatred a young sister has for her older brother. Couple it with the know-how to inflict sci fi retaliation and my palm's two-inch lifeline vies justification.

Only me, though. Not Rhys. She likes him. Respects him, too. Jerk!

Please, forgive me. I drifted. We can continue the tour if you wish? Cool.

Using a clock for directional purposes with 12 o'clock straight ahead, observe the things on pedestals starting at 2:00. First, the large Easy-Bake-turned-refrigerator she is converting for Pops. His idea of recycling. At 3:15, she has a holographic camera. At 4:30, a G.I. Joe doll on all fours kissing Barbie's plastic feet. At 7:38... Yo ho ho! What have we here?

This contraption has size, floodlights, foghorns and something like an infrared scanner. Swydni has no "SwydnInc. Merchandising" logo on it, yet, but there is a partially engraved description label on it: "SM1 Wall-Mounted Vi."

Vi? What on earth? Vi? Wall-mounted, even?

Nope, no clue.

Oh well, if I know Sis, providence unites me and this invention, like all of her mystery exploits. If not, scheduled break-ins will reveal the contraption's identity.

Let me see. Let me see. Fiddle with what? Fiddle with what?

As bewilderment over what surfaces as Vi's hand-held version strikes, a nip runs along the yellow streak in my back. Seldom do I expose my back to a door or window, especially in public places. This maneuver deterred some major misfortunes and lessened the severities of others. Ah, but the times I faux pas-ed permits this tingle's cognizance.

"What're you doing in my lab, Dinky?!"

Uh huh. Little sis. Sounds like her answering machine, too. Mean and loud.

"My door??" she trumpets. "What'd you do to my door?? And my security enforcers??"

She means those projectiles.

"Why's this funky, funky garment dangling on my camera??" yelling continuously.

"Funky, funky garment" translation: smelly, unsightly clothing.

"You touched my projects, too??" flipping her outer shirt aside as I run out of "scream" synonyms.

Swydni assesses the physical and mental damages yours truly infested upon her domain. Perchance, my brain ponders which experience history lends me, thus, allowing a way out of this mess?

No. I have different, useless thoughts, now. Almost pertinent to this situation, I wonder if Swydni made a people remote control. You know, something to adjust their volume or turn them off. Maybe imagination can help.

"Tell me, big bro, can amputation deter you from coming in here?!"

Click. Click. Click.

"'Do not disturb' signs don't work! You interpret 'Wrong Way' as come this way! High velocity salt pellets entice you to return with spiceless food! You even sent pictures of the trap door leading to Pops' den off to an amusement park for a new ride consideration! Tell me, what'll stop you??"

Click. Click. Nothing. Damn useless remote.

"You aren't paying attention, are you?!"

Maybe I should pay attention.

"Apparently, simple reminders don't cut it! Perhaps you need a behavior jolt!"

Oh, oh, oh! She thinks she has the upper hand? Good thing I have company. This brat distinctly requires an education on "strength in numbers." Are you with me? Uh... your... uh... response sounded muffled. You are my back-up, right? Huh? Huh?

Skip it.

"Little girl," smugly contending, "I... thought some dust fell in here. Since you despise grime..."

"Like yourself?"

"Ah ha, very funny," dropping the sarcasm. "Listen, chicklet, I wanted to show off your lab. Sue me."

"Show it off?" she puzzles. "Show it off to who?"

"Whom."

"That's what I wanna know."

"No, Swydni, the question is, 'show it off to whom?'"

"Whom is you, Dummy."

"Dinky!"

"Whomever."

Are horns sprouting up on her forehead?

"You're on my very last nerve! You're getting ejected!"

"You, little girl? Eject us?"

Before the statement left my lips, stupidity staked its claim on my forehead. Unless... unless you can jump in these pages?

Stop laughing.

Returning my concern to Swydni, her reaction reeks of predictability, not much unlike my ignorance. There she goes with her hands on hips, head tilted in the classic little sister angle, close eyes, sigh out of pity, look at me, snarl lip and say...

"'Us,' Dingy? Let me guess. You're doing that my-life's-a-book thing again, aren't you? Wake up and smell the psychiatrist. You're alone. In my lab. In trouble. BIG trouble!"

That last line was new. My fear? Not new. The last time she caught me in here, I ended up on a liquid diet. Anyway, a show of bravery could swing the pendulum my way.

"I can... scream for Pops."

"Even if he would bother to help you and despite the door's condition," she responds triumphantly, "my lab's soundproof. Comes in handy sometimes, don'cha think?"

Another angle, here. I need another angle.

Pondering another angle, it dawns on me: I outweigh her by a whole person and our height difference goes without mention. In fact, my shadow during an eclipse looms larger than her. How she intimidated me this long does not compute.

No longer! Today, she experiences "pain de Dinky!"

Standing at opposite ends of the lab, Swydni earnestly scans her immediate area. I study her and the situation at hand. Usually, she packs some weapon on her person.

Not for this occasion, though. She was wearing a big shirt that looked like one of mine.

Hey!

Anyway, she only claims a tank top and ultra skinny jeans as her immediate wardrobe. Thinking safety, or actually survival, an examination of her pants bares absolutely no chance whatsoever for a concealed weapon.

She has a dime in her pocket. I can read the date on it.

Enough observations. She looks ready for the showdown. Clint Eastwood-style, spaghetti western music appropriates the situation. I deduce Swydni has three feasible actions:

A. Dive left for the nearest weapon,

B. Get past me and employ an environmental weapon she installed for additional room security, or

C. Escape and plan my downfall another day.

We lock brains. A psycho psychic bond between us initiates the countdown at high noon.

Three. I confidently walk toward her. Eat your heart out, Clint.

Two. Still bridging the gap. Bridgework lingers in her near future.

One. A Taser??? How?? I never saw a bat belt! Besides, "none of the above" was not one of her options!

Okay, dude. Calm down. Reason my way out of this mess.

"Sis, darling! Can we talk like reasonable adults?"
>>ptzzzzzznk<<

"AAAAAAAAAAAAAAAAAAAAAAAAAAAAAAAAAAAAAAAAAAA
AAAAAAAAAAAAAAAAAAAAAAAAAAAAAAAAAAAAAAAAAAAAA
AAAAAAAAAAAAAAAAAAAAAAAAAAAAAAAAAAAAAAAAAAAAA
AAAAAAAAAAAAAAAAAAAAAAAAAAAAAAAAAAAAAAAAAAAAA
AAAAAAAAAAAAAAAAAAAAAAAAAAAAAAAAAAAAAAAAAAAAA
AAAAAAAAAAAAAAAAAAAAAAAAAAAAAAAAAAAAAAAAAAAAA
AAAAAAAAAAAAAAAAAAAAAAAAAAAAAgh!"

ooh. ow. discomfort.

All my life, pain has lived on me like an imaginary leach. It grew up on me fearing it may become blasé someday. Thus, pain always manifested itself in various intensities, wavelengths and body parts. I know pain. It helps distinguish this sucker from any other Other Guy.

This new pain has no casualness. Her beauty has knocked this grown man to his knees. Where have you been all my life and when are you leaving?

And the person who brought us together? She hovers like a teenage vulture. Domination and fury reflect in her face... and voice.

"Bridgework?"

Whoops. Forgot the bond.

"Why're you in my lab?"

"S-Sth-Sthwydni? The tae-ther?"

"You mean taser? I like it, too," she asserts with so much control. But the fury returns. "What were you doing in my lab?"

"Nothing. I merely w-w-w-wanted to thee your projects.

"Do ya think I'm stupid, Donkey?"

"Dinky!"

"Whatever," switching to sarcasm. "I'm getting tired of this scenario. For the last time, you won't come in my lab again, right?"

"O-o-of courthe not."

Meaning: until you leave again.

"You think I didn't hear that thought? Why don't we crank up the juice? Okay, big bro?"

"Nooooo!" Dang-blasted bond. "Y-y-your room ith off limiths!"

"I win?"

"Yeth!!! Pleeeeathe, thop Sthwydi! P-p-pleathe!"

She pauses a moment and reflects. A rather long moment from my standpoint.

"Uncle?"

"Uncle!!! Uncle!!! Oh, pleathe thop!"

"Say it again!"

"Uncle! Aunt! Niethe! Couthin twithe removed! Pleathe, Sthwydneeeeeeeeeeeeeee!"

The little wrench pauses again. The sounds of fibrillating jerkalations compound the tension. Finally, she turns off the volt-a-tron.

"Get out!" she spits.

Drying my face, stray current purées my internals. I crawl toward the door. Reaching the hall, I prepare for her traditional, baleful parting shots.

"As a reminder of where not to go, Dorky, let these electrodes hit you were the Good Lord split you."

"Woowoowhooooa!"

Con Ed Enemas. Ask for them by name. And, uh, why do my teeth feel an additional tingle all of a sudden?

"Stop pickin' on your sister, boy!"

It figures. From his den, he crackles to her defense. But who, tell me, who desperately tries using the mega killwatts to ride the rhythm into his own room, which he should have been in in the first place? Whose ion-enhanced senses can currently smell the asbestos right under his nose? Who lounges spread eagle and face down in the hallway, more energized than that doggone pink bunny? Who, dammit, who lies here...?

And lies here...?

And still lies here...?

Ahhh, the uncola. [sorry, obscure-product product placement]

And lies here until the body electric seriously dissipates? Like so...
"Gaaaaaah."

We can, >>spzzzt<<, conclude the tour with the final stop: my room.

Crawling upon my door, the extreme need to emit some liquid waste from sashaying kidneys is a number one concern.

Please, go in, keep your head up and sit down while I do this, uh, deed. First, I better find some grounding wire. Expect a little wait.

What? Grounding wire? Well, if you must know, whenever someone can voltagely compete with an electrical outstation when one goes to an outhouse, improper grounding petrifies the human transformer.

Trust me.

Surprisingly, few characters ever relieve themselves in books, television or the movies; ergo, my action best only take a line...

...or two to do. See? All done.

>>Krinch<<

Okay, I admit, the room could be a bit cleaner. For your own sake, though, pay no mind.

>>Krinch<< >>Kinch<< >>Krunch<<

Pay no mind. The offal that hides the wall-to-wall carpet masquerades as... motion detectors. Yeah.

>>Kinch<<

I could probably jump on the bed from here, I suppose.

>>Sssssshsh<<

Clean the bed. Trust me, the bed gets a cleaning date. Anyway, you did notice the many adornments decorating my walls? I am winding down the final conversion from adolescence. At least, that excuse defends the Muppet Babies poster... and the Gonzo puppet... and the Miss Piggy telephone... and... never mind.

Post your peepers over here at this wall where mature representations embellish. These bookshelves used to house "revealing" magazines. Pops confiscated and pitched them in the fireplace, saying they make great kindling. He also said using the right wood – obvious pun – lets the smoke resemble the model's curves and... curves. Now, my shelves hold memorabilia from the days of the educational institute, i.e., high school yearbooks.

>>Sfwish<<

Huh? My bed? Leaking? No, the waterbed ran away months ago. Now, where was I?

All male freshmen at Carlisle High had to try out for football as some part of a macho, pubertic ritual. In the summer prior to my freshman year, the rites of passage into manhood forgot my address.

No height, no width, little depth, but plenty of heart. The heart propelled me into a duel for the starting quarterback position.

I remember breaking from the huddle during practices, walking to the line and placing my hands on the underside of the center's privates. Nobody barked out plays with the intensity my vocal cords cracked. Yeah, the voice quivered in its attempts to grow bass, coincidentally, at the same time Pops' voice quivered to go soprano. He had just been put out of football, thus the pigskin tradition naturally passed down to me.

The starting QB position was mine to lose. Barely able to see the defense over the center's buttocks, I disappeared from my would-be tacklers once the ball hiked and the melee of young, steroided muscles danced, stirring the field's topsoil. Launching a bomb from deep within the brown cloud, the football always landed softly in a speedy receiver's hands right before he got knocked parallel. Two weeks before the first game, the last receiver bit the dust in a Gatorade accident, forcing me to resort from arm strength to leg strength.

My social liability – no height – transformed into my best football asset. Instead of propelling the offense with efforts above the gridiron, I chauffeured it with darts and dashes, inside, outside and under the men-mountains. Each successful scrimmage dipped my rival, Durdy Redd, from Coach Mad's favor. Redd fell all the way back to fourth-string defensive deepback.

One week before our first game, practice went routinely. Coach informed the press earlier that day that the road to a future state championship started in my driveway.

High acclaims for a short freshman. More anger fuel for Durdy. Again, practice went routinely until... until I called my favorite play:

Bulldoze right/tri-op/daylight.

In laymen's terms, the offensive linemen bury the defensive line away from the right, I roll right with the tailback for option one: a pitch. Option two: throw to the receiver running for daylight. Unfortunately, all of our receivers could only wheelchair to daylight.

Running the ball myself represented option three. Choosing option three, I parted all immediate obstacles and the tailback blocked the first secondary one. Recalling the defensive layout in my mind, only two players remained between me and the end zone. A snappy juke lets me pickpocket the next-to-last defender's shorts right off him and into the path of my last sucker.

Durdy!

Surprise.

If I scored, Durdy would plummet so far down in Coach's eyes, he could mistake him for phlegm.

First impulse gyrated my hips in preparation for another neck-poppin' juke.

No! Durdy required a cleat planted through his chest, unwantingly volunteering himself as the welcome mat to TD Mansion.

If only he had cooperated.

Instead, without any warning whatsoever, Durdy bulleted his entire 6'2", 165-pound frame into the space between my solar plex and bellybutton. At the last possible moment, I tried forearming him. I revived in the ambulance to the paramedics' argument over how fingers grew from my lower ribs.

My sophomore season ended before it started, too. One week before the season opener, my closet lacked one particular article of clothing. Durdy, fearing he may lose his quarterback position, corrected my wardrobe deficiency, accommodating me with plaster pants for any ensemble.

Despite the hysterical, sobbing protests of Coach Mad, Durdy transferred the following year. Still spurned by the coach's comments about me right before our freshman season, he moved in with my brother and enrolled at Carlisle's arch-rival, South Peazy High. He won two state championships for them. He later went on to have a multi-million-dollar professional football career.

Jerks!

Seriously believing the football injuries forecasted more sport-related hardships, and despite Durdy's detour, my junior year issued an introduction to student politics. Student Body President, or popularity poll, asked any junior or senior if s/he would catalyst the pupilage into a lean, mean, teacher's pet machine. It also improved one's image, if one's image quested improvement.

Moving at mach-one, I fulfilled all requirements and actually felt the election delayed my inevitable victory. I even thought voting for myself would be a waste of energy.

The final count showed my defeat by a single landslide.

The presidency again yearned for this idiosyncratic my senior year. I refused to suffer another embarrassment. Nonetheless, the job called:

"Please, Dinky, take me. We could reshape this school," it said. "Nobody can do what you can."

It meant nobody wanted to do what I can.

Nobody ran for president. The faculty ended up selecting a nobody for president. Some nameless dweeb who went from sewer-level approbation to legendary high school fame. A dweeb whose name remains a mystery, but always answered to, "Yo, Prez."

My vocation in secondary education: extreme peak possibilities, extreme valley dwelling.

After high school, I went to college, recently picked up a degree and got a job. I am currently on vacation and do not wish to expand on it. It does explain how my rent gets paid, though.

I live at home, because I tolerate my parents better than most heirs care to. The college dorm life made me appreciate the Momma-Poppa-Swyd frat house. It almost made Mom's cooking less homesickening, too. A little, not much.

These chapters of my history serve a purpose. Without understanding where one has been as an individual, when one stands on earth's passageway to the beyond, they look back on circular, redundant flashbacks. A literal o.o.b.e. déjà vu... vu.

These personal reflections reaffirm good things should appear in the future tense, simply because they pepper the past. I either failed the recognition or the manipulation of those happenings clearly dangling from life's carrot-on-a-stick.

Which brings us to the literal present. The up-to-date, now, contemporary, vogue, currently, what-the-goings-on-are. This point marks history's passage and the future's emergence for The Other Guy, using each to compliment the other and themselves.

Mark.

Remember the story about Pops and his tofu? No? How about the "reminder" he ordered? Well, check out the glass hieroglyphic. The glass hieroglyphic in full sprint stride.

Recall: Pops' father-aided lateral velocity exceeded my forward drive.

It might have helped if he threw me low, letting me use the floor to run on. He did toss me low enough to dodge the ceiling fan.

Nice guy, that Oscar.

Somehow, Pops found energy efficient, break-a-way glass, believing my temper, stupidity and forgetfulness would all challenge him again. Even if they got together, he could never duplicate that soaring pose. Swinging arms and swaying legs represent variables. Incorporating flight fright makes for an unduplicatable equation. Unless...

Mmmaybe he could throw me through the Egyptian-posed plexiglas squarely. Anything is possible, especially if I can reshape my body to the mold.

Approaching the window, stepping into the "foot" of it, I attempt the obtuse. You can always...

"Uhnnn."

tell when extra poundage...

"Ummphf."

visits your waistline when window sills...

"Grrr."

no longer fit the way designers fashioned them to.

"Yesss!"

A little snug in the chest, but still wearable.

Proving the pointless, de-clothing this "attire" tops my to-do list. If somebody sees me...

Too late!

Somebody prowls the backyard. And not just an ordinary somebody, either. Simply the most beautiful somebody ever seeing me commit a stupid act. A utility company's somebody. A utility company's somebody, laughing at me. Wait... not laughing at me... smiling at me.

There is a difference. Trust me. I know.

Whoa. A beautiful woman smiling at me. At me! At me... in a window, >>schmlok<<, out of the window and... >>ktoom<<, on the sticky floor.

Regaining something close to composure, I lay there astonished that she smiled at me. She did smile at me. Oh, and what a smile! Those beautiful, original teeth, and her beautiful, raven hair with a touch of curl, and her beautiful face, and her bee-you-tea-full body! Never have utility clothes draped over a worker with such zeal and desire. I bet they hang in her locker praying she comes to work on time.

I would. Taking up at least two or three hooks.

Finally standing, I vision the vision disappear into the shrubbery between the yards. I managed a last glance at her tool belt. It sends envious thoughts of the screwdriver through this non-master mechanic.

I need to sleep on this. Actually, I want to sleep on her. Or maybe sleep with her, then, a couple seconds later, hold her and smoke a cigarette. Oh, if she could only read *my* meters.

>>Yawwwwn<<

Yeah, I need to sleep on this. From the looks of the storm clouds relaxing overhead, the sandman should have no problem with me. Hopefully, the meter reader can get her work done before the rain comes. Picturing her in a moist uniform, though, does have serious... NO! If my Conscience comes to, sleep may not become me.

>>Rrrrmblrumble<<

Yeah. As if the weather will actually help me sleep.

If you promise not to steal anything or touch me, ahem, you can stay until I wake up in the following chapter.

>>Krench<<

I could jump to the bed from here, I suppose. Good night.

SUBSEQUENT CHAPTER

Peace. Total, uninhibited peace. No griefs, no hardships, no diet cola aftertaste.

Peace.

The kind of peace that comes while viewing a coastal sunrise. The sun awakens, burroughing its way from the sand blanket Sister Night tucked him into. Picture it as the morning light nudges the little stars aside as if to say, "the basketball court is mine."

Peace.

The kind of peace the rich spend goo-gobs of money achieving through recreation or the utmost disposal of their enemies.

Peace.

The ultimate equilibrium of mind, body and spirit. The unbridled bliss achieved by... sleep. The poor man's vacation.

"Excuse me."

Although reserved for anyone, sleep gives all, despite their bank account, the capability...

"Excuse me, Author. You may have disguised your voice by slanting the letters, but who else could it be? Need I remind you of our deal: I live my life on my own. Now, if you want to do me a favor, find a publisher, but let me live my life. In the event something prevents me from offering substantial verbiage for this literary reflectance on my existence, then, and only then, can you choreograph me all the live-long day."

If that's the case, Dinky, look behind you.

"Puh-leeze. Do you honestly expect me to fall for that old trick?"

Okay, but remember who you are.

"The Other Guy. So what?"

So... what should an Other Guy think if he felt the sudden wind gush you're feeling?

"Who knows? A speeding I-beam, maybe?"

Good guess.

"Guess, smess, you idiota! I happen to be dreaming."

Then humor this Spanish idiot. Turn around.

"Okay, whatever. Oh. Goodness. A speeding I-beam. Coming my way. Eye-high."

Remember who you are.

Huh? Nawww. Nobody gets hurt when they dream. Besides... how can I get knocked unconscious while I am slee– >>Pwang<<

Oooooooh. That's gotta smart. He's seeing enough stars to start his own constellation.

As much as slumping beauty gets subjected to, wouldn't you think The Other Guy deserves a break? A divergence from the routine? A migration of the todays and yesterdays before embarking on the same ol' tomorrows?

And here it comes.

His break currently slinks into his dream's dream of a dream. A simply sensual silhouette sways Dinky's way. Call it the fate he couldn't give himself, but those curves look familiar and they want Dinky. Fantasy-shine unzips the form's shadow mask, uncovering the beauty and identity of this vision. It's the meter reader and she really wants Dinky. She bends down to awaken the misfit from I-beam slumber. He revives, taking her into his arms.

Virginity begone, he thinks. Even if it's a dream, his peace has delivered the piece he's craved for far too long.

Unfortunately, storm clouds bring this dude back to his present.
>>Kra-BOOOMM-kkkktz<<

"Wha–? Huh? Nooooooooooooo! Yo, yo, Author, take me back! Author... Sandman... Mr. I-beam... somebody take me back up. Please, please, pretty please!"

Nothing. Damn.

Why, why, why, why, why, why can I not finish a dream? A nightmare, though? I stay asleep long enough to catch the credits.

Well, something tells me facing my current reality outweighs any nocturnal body suspension.

Without a doubt, thunder scares me. This tidbit explains why the ceiling fan right now holds my body tight. Reflexively speaking, Mother Nature's static cling spring-loads my muscles, propelling me skyward when I sleep. Swydni apparently took full advantage of my heavy hibernate, donning me in velcro pajamas.

Her river of revenge runs deep.

Oscillating at twelve feet, I look outside whenever the window swings by and mull over what the thunder heralded. Other than the clouds – which block the sun, which promote the gloom, which invigorate the humdrums – thunder heralds the rinsing agent. Cleaning more than the filth street sweepers tend to leave behind, the herald reminds of biblical history. The history of the covenant stemming from it and an opportunity for bathing if you forgot to pay your water bill.

Rain.

Webster says rain is, 1, water falling in drops from clouds; 2, a shower or outpouring of anything.

Amazing how "Dinky Definitions" differ so greatly from the norm:

1. I remember blissful times. Memories of an oh-too-seldom impotent Pops and myself watching the rain, lawn-chair lounging in the garage. We would just sit there, not saying much. Enjoying each other's unperturbed company, intermissions took place where we came close to solving world peace and the taste great/less filling debates. More often than not, he bounced me to the closest puddle as a casual reminder of who stood above whom.

2. Rain also reminds me. It reminds me of my personal cloud's expandabilities. When this "cloud" has absorbed enough hardship moisture, it comes down, down, down.

3. Turkey farmers run the fear of losing their entire crop in downpours. Turkeys, in their paltry intelligence, are confounded by the droplets. Wondering where these liquid bombs originate, they look up with their mouths open and drown. Stupid animals.

Each interpretation suits me well. The one with the best fit? Without a doubt... gobble, gobble.

But perhaps, I judge myself much too harsh. Perhaps, I admit defeat before the contest begins. Perhaps, this segment runs too long.

Unhinging myself from the ceiling fan, >>tchtttchittchichcht<<, I thank the mess on my bed for its shock-absorption characteristics and make my way to "The Closet."

>>Kinch<< >>Kunch<< >>Kinch<< >>Kunch<< >>Kinch<< >>Kunch<<

Giving yourself the period between chapters to observe my room, did you notice no socks, underwear, garments, or etc., commingle with the filth at foot level? The walk-in closet unveils my favoritism for wardrobe.

Voilà! An organizational system uniquely uncommon for a young, single male.

Clothes do not, and will not, arbitrarily hang wherever the hanger made contact with the suspense bar. No. Each clothing item conforms to a predesignated area according to apparel, color and wearing favorability.

For example: ties... naw, too simple.

For example: suits are staged furthest from the door, because I like wearing them most. Similar to meat stationed in the back of a grocery store, the selector bypasses less desired items or items to compliment the intended meat, thus prompting the selector into selecting those less desired or complimentary items.

Another grocer philosophy lends itself in my closetal layout. I prefer dark colors like most people prefer name-brand items over the cheapies. Less popular brands are not as profitable, overall, to the grocer, thus the more profitable, brand name/popular items get better shelf space. In a similar manner, the favored darker colors get better positioning than happy colors.

Shirts and pants have separate housing areas, reducing the uni-suit mating factor. Solid-colored articles precede multi-colored ones, using their dominant color for co-ordinance. Shoes have the sport/casual/semi-formal/formal/dress-to-kill placement order. Sweaters get folded and t-shirts, entering my wardrobe only as gifts, tend to get recycled into emergency toilet paper.

Anyway, one clothing storage error I never commit concerns wire hangers.

Yuck.

Wire hangers put ugly humps in suits and shirts. Pants folded on them contract unsightly creases at the fold.

Double yuck.

Use hangers specially made for the attire they support. Especially pants! Treat your clothes right and they return the favor. Which, by the way, segues perfectly into drawerology and washology. Two scientific discussions reserved for an audiobook, perhaps?

So, recalling how clouds obstructed the proper interpretation concerning the time of day, I cannot possibly dress accordingly. The time of day factors great importance in choosing correct attire. Alas, life gives instructions to a law everyone should live by: if you have a question... ask.

"Smavic? Time."

A computer-generated voice announces the earth's universal and axial position in relation to my placement within the dominion of continental America.

"Two-fifty-seven p.m. Wednesday."

Smavic, you ask? Another product of SwydnInc. Merchandising, I answer. The SM4000 Audio/Visual Interactive Chronometer.

Smavic.

Swydni offers various Smavic models with selective attitudes. She gave me the basic prototype, because... because...

Why *did* she give it to me?! Out of love, maybe? To show her appreciation for verifying the Oscar/Kath E DNA combo?

Puh-leeze! If I know better, you should.

This mystery seeks future investigation. I should store it in the dank corners of my mind, where it will inevitably be forgotten.

Where was I?

Ahhh, yes. What to wear? What to wear?

Since I wore the grey, double-breasted hamburger yesterday, with shoes I fail to understand, today I should wear something... like... yes! A

Ragú, soft purple, paisley, mock collar button-up and... oh yes! A Piggly Wiggly store brand, stonewashed, black, relaxed-fit jeans and... oh my! Casual cool, leather loafers that bring extra notoriety to the socks:

Sparkling neon.

These socks' color depends on how the light reflects. They seldom match each other, although they generally match something else on my body. They also help catalyst feminine conversation.

Yes! I will do anything to get their attention.

You know, I had forgotten this is a book, thus allowing me to skip ahead to another scene without physically going through the motions of getting dressed, sullying my shoes amongst the wall-to-wall, deep plush rubbish, being allured into Swydni's room, etc. Also, it lets me avoid Mom and Pops when I sneak out.

Anyway, the scene changes to Russell's front yard as our hero, ahem, advances toward the front door. A nice door, too. Putting my ear against it and...

>>Nok<<

Yep! The Wilson Pinnacle Portal. Criss-crossed hardwoods with a three-inch ivory core. I bet it took some serious effort to install this.

I hear... voices. Womanish.

Uh oh, here comes somebody. Back up and look natural.

>>Smik<<>t-chit<<>>chank<<

Hmmm. A SecuriTech chain/deadbolt superlock system set.

The door opens and... Damn! Why me?

"Hi, Mrs. Russell. How are you feeling today?"

" ."

"Good. Glad to hear it. You do look" – lie, Dinky, lie – "very, uh, nice. Yeah. Nice. Is Russell home?"

" ."

Her tone of face seldom invites me. Thankfully, this situation has repeated itself enough for comfortability to settle in.

" ," her pupils remark. My cue to mosey on before she blinks.

"Thank you, ma'am. I can find my way."

Slipping past her steadfast pillage, an odd enrapture tantalizes my nasal follicles. Mrs. Russell epitomizes garage sale wear. Bad garage sale wear. Sincerely doubling as my personal equal-yet-opposite wardrobe reaction, the special hanger she must use for her soot suit makes me honestly jealous I never bought one. What actually astounds me, though, is the unmistakable scent of Par Fùmé.

Bottled fragrances rank as much importance as grooming in regards to proper appearance. The undeniable $82-a-milliliter bouquet compliments any ensemble. Question is, who has it?

Mrs. Russell?

Puh-leeze. She has a sign posted on her front window that reads, "Beware of Me."

Getting past her, the perfume thought, like most other thoughts, vacate the residential like prom night teenagers at the local snooze-here/booze-here/lose-it-here motel. Nevertheless, I feel her dilate seething holes into my invertebrate as I make my way upstairs to Russell's room.

Uncomfortable? Me?

Yes! Like a woman with unretouched breasts in a beauty pageant.

Cautiously making it up the spiral steps, I hang a right and walk the length of a major hallway to arrive at the open bedroom doorway of...

"Russell! Wut up?"

" ," he responds, steadily working at his computer station.

Although like-mother-like-son, I can smelt him for his ignore-ance.

Approaching him nonchalantly, I prepare a heaping helping of knuckles, smothered in hollanDink sauce. Bon appet–

"Whulp!"

He moved? I missed? Fortunately, momentum carries me over his lap. Unfortunately, not fast enough to elude a spank.

Nearing floor, I tuck, rolling on my shoulder until centrepically roosting on my feet. Russell hydraulically straightens his reclining position before standing to confront me.

Circling each other, strategies strangely float into my head from the left and float out on the right. Surmising the "A-ha" theory that ideas instantly pop into one's head is bull, I believe these strategies suspend themselves, waiting to merge with human brain activity. Proving this hypothesis, I reverse direction.

A-ha! Now, strategies float in from the right and placing a finger in my left ear keeps them there. My battle course has a plan. The only problem is this last paragraph of pure bowel made me forget the real task at hand. Maybe Russell can help.

"Uh, Russell? What are we doing?"

" ."

I really hate it when he talks like that.

"Russell, stop walking around and..."

" ?"

"Oh, really?"

" !"

"Hey, bud. Those are fighting winks."

Circling each other, strategies strangely float into my head from the left and float out on the right. Surmising this same scene recently took place, I instead call upon history for assistance. Here comes the fax:

For years, he has welcomed me in his room in this manner. Never really taking inventory, he surely has thousands of dollars in hi-tech merchandise; none of it ever damaged, either. Staring across and down at him, a few things will change. Assuming a toro stance, I charge the matadwarf, forecasting to break him or a belonging.

Bracing for contact, he... he sidesteps me! Putting his hand on the back of my neck, he pushes down, sending me head first into a Persian rug. Sliding to a stop, I finally mess up something of his, but leave myself in a three-point stance with knees and face as the contact points with the floor. Not only a comical position, the ideal position for a...

>>Boot<<

"Get up."

Monotone as they were, Russell's first words would carry more weight had he not forced me to put extra crimps in his rug.
I spring up, growling, ready for the climax. Within arm's length of each other, we prove it.

My favorite punch, the left hook. His, the right jab. Both disbursed at amazing velocity. At the moment jussst before impact, the thrusts terminate. Hands unfold. We dust off the evidence of today's fray from one another and "dap": front-swinging our hands to appear we will slap them together in the normal urban-style greeting ritual. At the well-practiced prior-point-of-impact, we separate our fingers, allowing them to weave through one another's. Then we close our hands and backswing our fists to collide them.

Dap.

"G'day, Dink," he cordially relates.

"Top of the noon, my friend," retreating to rest my buns as he returns to his computer.

Barely distanced from him, I start wondering. Normally, we conclude these "greetings" with near jocularity, politely tucking away our aggressions. If we ever went as far as actually crowning a victor, I would permanently be court jester.

No. Not anymore.

Sparks of rage collect within, culminating into a tower of torment. Yes. A new ruler shall reign. Long live DinKing.

Spinning hard, bringing a right hook harder, today's hallmark confrontation will have a different...

"Aieeeeeeee!"

"You scream funny, Dink."

Where did he...

"Where did you get that sword???"

"I thought you'd try something, so I ordered it."

Staring down at the weapon and the fencer, I think the jester's outfit could be ideal for fall fashions.

He withdraws and heads back to his computer. Turning away, more humbly than before, his clairvoyance astounds me. Or was he just lucky? I again wonder, spinning to strike.

"Aieeeeeeee!"

"Actually, Dink, it's a "Swiss Army Phlegm Extractor." The mailman dropped it off about 20 minutes ago."

What? Twenty min–? Order? Swiss Arm–? No! The greater the brain activity, the bigger the hemorrhage.

"Don't worry, Dink. You can fashionably wear green and red checks when the leaves change."

Huh? How did...? No! A stroke cometh.

Turning away, thrice humble than before, a soft chair pillows my thinking. Trying to relax and observe my buddy's new project, a stroke possibility increases. It escalates more and more, becoming almost rhythmic and... twangy? Of course, I know better, but the cause of my Excedrin Headache stems from noises masquerading as country music.

"Russell? That noise?"

"Whaddaya think it is?" answering without beholding.

"My parents on The Nashville Network's Bathtub Hour."

"Close. It's a song I'm putting together. Interested?"

"No!"

Body language answered, too. Yeah, as if it all mattered. He grossly bypasses my implied plea for no more information on this topic.

"'My Truck Cheated on Me and My Wife Broke Down in Texas.' You like?"

>>Sigh<<

He makes his money this way. Ideas hit him and he grows them to financial harvest. Bushels and bushels and bushels. I used to think he and his mother came into a great deal of money from Mr. Russell's life insurance, who died about the same time Pops' brother did.

NO! I know for a fact Pops' brother had no children.

Russell rarely talks about his father and you understand how he could afford to live in this remarkable house, although his mother has no semblance of employment. This idea... this song... will crop riches on the title alone.

My feelings on the whole thing...?

"I hate it!"

"Good," appearing to take stock in my response. "Then it's a winner."

When will I learn? What will I learn?

In all the years of our friendship, we seldom have talks offering any type of sustenance. Possibly, my subconscious reaps the bountiful fruit that underlie the primer of hollow conversation. The conscious mind surely gets nada.

"C'mere, Dink. I wanna show you something."

Taking a load off my mind, I stroll across the large room, kicking a few more crimps in the Persian rug before standing behind the seated Einstein. He holds a magazine page depicting a man in his forties, aimlessly staring straight ahead.

"You see this bald man?"

"Yeah," I reply. "So what?"

"Watch as I scan this and punch up the image. There!"

"I repeat, so what?"

"Keeping the original image on the top of the screen, let's split it in half and put the right side in the right, lower corner and vice versa with the left. Now, if I duplicate the right side of his face and flip it to create a new left side... like thus..."

"Oh, man!"

"And repeat the process for the former left half of his face..."

"You created two new faces which hardly resemble the original. How?"

"Because few people's faces are actually symmetrical."

"But why use a bald man?"

"How many men part their hair in the middle?"

"Pops."

Dead silence.

Most people would face their conversationalist, offering no less than an expression of sympathy. Not Russell. When we talk, he always stares straight ahead, unless something arrested his attention prior to our normally senseless chats.

Looking at Russell's monitor, I wonder, er, speculate how the asymmetrical phenomenon occurs. Then I recall reading about how many people chew their food on one side of their mouth. It builds up the muscles on that side of their face more than the other side. Oh, that reminds me...

"Russell, where do you keep your tongue when you eat?"

Pause. A long pause.

Although impossible, I swear he "cut" his eyes around inside his head, staring daggers at me through his ear.

"In a glass saucer along with the gum I was chewing," he tallies.

Assuming seriousness over sarcasm, due to today's uncharted medical breakthroughs, a fashionable thought flits over me.

"Knowing you own more than one of anything, how many tongues do you have? Do you color coordinate or contrast with your gums?"

Another pause. No problem. I wanted some concentration when taking inventory of his belongings. But breaking my attentiveness from Russell immediately allows the twangs to reestablish its assault:

Myyyyyyyyyyy truck cheated on me and muh wife broke down in Texas.

My Chevy found anuther ta give its stick shift to.

And as muh wife lay crumpl'n, needin' a new transmission...

I found muhself a wonderin', pond'rin' what I miss mo'

"Russell! Kill the song!"

Myyyyyyyyyyy truck cheated on me and muh wife broke down in Texas.

"Russell!!! Kill!!! The!!! Song!!!"

The dang fo'-by-fo'

>>click<<

"Thank you," breathing exhaustedly from the musical assault. "Thank you very much."

Pause. What the...

"If you're bored and, uh, spent, Dink..."

Why the pauses?

"...go get something to drink."

Again, why the pauses?

"You know your way around the kitchen, don't you?"

"I think so."

"Well, there's plenty of room."

"For a house this size... Hold it! Room for what?"

He fluctuates his eyes as if totally confused or taken back by something. A rhetorical look creases his brow.

"You're dense."

"No," recalling chats with Swydni. "Dink."

"Go ahead, Dink," talking almost resigned. "Go ahead."

Now, confusion osmoses me. I think Russell tried to tell me something, but what? What could or would he try to say? Anyway, heading out of his room, another thought flashes.

"Russell, what do you feed Apocalypse?"

He perks. Ecstatic that I... spoke to him again? Who knows? What is his problem?

"It's about time, Dink!"

"About time? For what?"

"That you... wait a minute. Why'd you ask about Apocalypse's food?"

"Ummm, it... it, like, just came to me. For some reason, that thought crossed my mind."

"Oh," again resigned.

"Who let the air out of your balloon?"

"You, my friend."

"Russell," not catching the meaning of his statement, "what do you feed the dog?"

I obviously partake in this conversation on the superficial level.

"Canned meat with potato chunks," he sighs.

"Hash?"

"I don't do drugs, Dink."

"No, no, no. Corn beef hash. For Apocalypse. You feed Apocalypse corn beef hash."

Saying that last line crystallizes it.

"You feed Apocalypse corn beef hash?"

"So."

"I eat corn beef hash!"

"So."

"So. So. So, it looks like dog food!"

"With potato chunks, Dink."

"Yeah," chuckling, "with potato chunks."

"And you eat it."

"And I... Hey!"

"What?"

"Are you funning me?"

"Would I?"

Dead silence. Just stares.

"Dink, believe me, your well-being lists as a major concern of mine. I wouldn't fun you. I owe you."

"Really," not remembering when he borrowed any money from me. "How much?"

"Not money."

"Then what are you talking about?"

"More."

"More than money?"

"Forget it," giving me the look like someone gives a car desperately needing a tune up. "Someday it'll all come to pass."

"Okay, Russell. Whatever."

On that note, I head out of his bedroom and towards the kitchen. Reaching the stairs, Russell leans out of his doorway.

"Somebody'll eat more than hash, if you catch my drift."

Was he trying to tell me something significant, again?

Refusing to let his words slow my decent [on the stairs], I touchdown, sniffing for pots and pans. Pot and pans, you ask? No. Not food contained in them. The pots and pans themselves. Having a few of those metal babies in real, real, real close approximation to my nose permanently implanted its unique aroma upon my odorous database. Although pots and pans carrying different brand names carry different scents, they all have a base smell.

>>Sniff<< >>Sniff<<

One problem fine-tuning an ability for a specific task, it cancels out other bodily abilities. Sight, hindering me from watching where I travel. Touch, which is fine, because I feel nothing I run into. Taste, no comment. And etc. When the task is done and the abilities return one at a time, I find myself at my intended destination.

"Whoa!!! What a kitchen! The Jetsons would die for this!"

This kitchen creates wide-eyed amusement each and every time. Complete and total wide-eyed amusement. Each and every time.

The ears come on-line, detecting a low decibel gurgle. They try relaying the information brainwardly. Unfortunately, the ogles hoard the thought processor with the awesome display of Russell's fabulous kitchen. The gurgle grows to a throaty growl. Most semi-intelligent people would add two and two, equating trouble lurks nearby. Me? This throaty growl creates wonderment of why my stomach groans.

Did I eat? Did Mom cook it? No and... no. Am I hungry? Not really. Does my stomach really want any profuse provisions? No, not exactly. Does my coherence skew barren galaxies? Oh, yeah! Definitely!

"Grrrrrr."

Grrrrrr? Hmmm. I wonder what... Hold it! Two plus two?

Four!

Damn!

I slowly tilt my head down. Slowly, I focus the visuals and slowly, I see potential pain staring wantonly at my groin.

"Hi, Apocalypse."

Hopefully, the sweetness in that statement gives this mutt diabetes.

"How are you today, Apocalypse?"

More sugar. Moooore sugar.

Surpassing the best subwoofer on the market, Apocalypse releases another, "grrrrrr." Sweat sends my face all aglow. I can see this dog picturing my testicles hanging from his rearview mirror. All hell will break loose soon.

Not once has the dog diverted its eyes from my reproductive jewels. Thus, the opening steel trap with gums sanctions the bulls-eye that suddenly appears on my button fly.

Normally, few things hinder me from painting my life with words. Continued descriptions of the tongued black hole, though, can have serious repercussions. Ergo, this rooster need not go to Switzerland for gender reassessment.

"Haahrrummmph."

Apocalypse chomps at my groin. Conscience. I barely dodge its attack, signified by the fact that the dog currently spits my buttons... into a spittoon?

Oh yeah, a surefire cue to leave.

I run for the back door.

Yes! The back door! Remember the ivory core?

Completing this mission requires a jaunt around the island in the kitchen, rounding the corner into the utility room and a mad dash through the back foyer. Will thunder pooch, who fancies converting my buttocks into a drive-thru, permit it?

Leaving the starting blocks, the first obstacle provides no problem. Apocalypse corners on a dime and is not far behind. In fact, I feel its hot breath on my behind. It feels pretty good.

I hug the next turn into the utility room. Apocalypse hugs it harder. The dog must sport steel-belted radial paws.

An inter-organ-ization communiqué memos the brain to stop thinking. It points out how the mind closes down if too many ideas get inside at once.

The "mad dash" point approaches. Apocalypse remains too close. The dog will, undoubtedly, catch me within the last twenty yards. Oh, did I mention Russell has a huge house?

Dammit. Another thought. Another memo.

I kick in the turbo booster, but, presumably, a bald flea with a French accent instructs Apocalypse to engage warp factor six.

The dog's warp engines power up as I reach for a serving cart. Throwing it in the dog's path, the fur monster goes right through it, slowing only by a sliver. Hopefully, Mrs. Russell understands the damage my presence does to her home.

Dagnabbit! Another thought!

Ten yards from the door and I am home free! Just then, another thought flows in: Where is Russell?

That did it! My head posts a condemned sign, I stop dead in my tracks and turn around. Apocalypse, steadily charging, smiles. Shocked by the act of a smiling dog, I try counting his teeth. He cranks open his jaws and dives for me. Good. I can count his back teeth first.

My brain suddenly reboots under new management, screaming something about getting intimate with the carpet. Gravity takes the initiative, reaching up and yanking my face into the stain-resistant anso. Actually, gravity sucked my head down harder than I prefer. My nose bounced a few times and discovered Mrs. Russell scrimped on the padding. Anyhow, this maneuver costs less blood than Apocalypse would have sprinkled from me. Speaking of the Kill-9, he sails over me, lands on all fours and pivots with feline perfection right in the doorway.

My exit? Blocked!

Apocalypse roars and charges. I whimper and wince.

We renew our chase scene. Oh, by the way, have you inspected Russell's house, yet? Well, since distancing the front door requires some travel time, a very quick tour of the lower level can happen. Hope you can speed read, because the mammal munch monster still has the mads for my mutton.

Utility room... kitchen... living room... dining room... down the mini-steps and...

Whoa! This room *still* has room! I should slow down and soak in the magnificence.

"RrrrrWarfff!!!"

I should speed up and soak in the magnificence!

The ceiling must be twenty feet. The balconies are way cool. Oh man, the plants. A glass door. If I can just...

"Garrrrmmmmph!"

Next visit. We can do whatever on the next visit.

It seems Apocalypse refuses to list "residential travel agent" as a career choice. Regardless, I cannot help but to forever admire this room. Coming up on a... a... an entertainment system from hell. Is that new? Good golly, what a house! Breathtaking!

"Hrrrrrrr!"

Life-taking! I need an exit and a second wind.

Nearing lap one, I see more mini-steps. Go up into the... foyer? Foyer. Front door! Front door number eight!

"The wood journey." Am I ready? Well, an ounce of prevention prevents a pound of pain. That means a system diagnostic is in order. Please, let it show a bunch of ounces.

This is Dinky Control, deep with the brain centers of the host. The thought of a television show based here, presented on The Fox Network, seems feasible. Well, it did at one time. But so anyway, let the immediate situation undergo conclusion. All Apocalypse-related systems: report!

Primary Frontorial Skin Sensors here, Control. Operational and ready.

Secondary Subversive Sensors to Control: Below normal Adrenaline levels, but functional.

Speedometer Index reporting in. Sufficient velocity exists for upcoming operation, although, more Adrenaline may allow an experimental phase through the door.

Control to Speedometer Index: Do what you can with what you have. Pain Inhibitors? What is your status?

Inadequate Adrenaline for masking discomfort past the two-second mark, Control.

Control to Adrenaline: Adrenaline? Adrenaline? Where is Adrenaline?

Shields here, Control. I saw Adrenaline at the bar, drinking with captains of oil tankers.

Thank you, Shields. What is your condition?

Extra absorbent with wings to prevent unsightly stains, Control.

Not Panty Shields! Defense Shields!

Defense Shields here with arms over the face, dude. Totally situated.

Control to Buttock Sensors: Where is Apocalypse?

Preparing to taste test me, Control!

Control to Speedometer Index: Put those bunions to work! All systems: prepare for impact in three-point-two yards. This is Dinky Control returning control to Dinky Main.

Duh... what a house! Okay, okay, okay. Climb steps, start countdown and get ready to hit through the door.

Three.

Two.

One.

>>qra-CHOOOOM<<

"Yessssss!"

The exhilaration of approaching such a barrier, not entirely certain the task of surpassing it will happen, gives an ultimate sense of accomplishment once succeeded. When that barrier splinters and the fragmented "trophies" air-dance and spasm on the land behind you, what else other than delirium multi-breeds throughout your heart and soul. If only the system diagnostic confirmed an important ingredient to make the feelings last.

Dinky Control to Dinky Main: Adrenaline quit. Prepare for radical cessation of all motor functions due to pain overload, effective immediately.

"Aaaaaaaaarrrrrg... oomph!!!"

The scream terminates. Ceased by a large human body losing balance while maintaining its forward thrust. Think about it like a grand piano rolling down a steep San Francisco street. It approaches peak velocity right when a leg crumples. Like said piano, I tumble, stumble and bumble through Russell's yard... across my gravel driveway... and upon our august foliation before, >>th'mok<<, coming to rest.

Groping Ms. Tree like nouveau, horny art, I wait. I wait a long time. I wait a long time upside down. I wait for my family of senses to collect upon me like the children they are.

Going through ebony-colored wood and ivory upsets more than Stevie Wonder. It hurts! It really hurts!

Funny, though, all these years of woe rarely amounted to hospitalization. Believe me, I have a room at the Hospital Hilton. Suite E.R. I just seem to visit it less often than regular people. Regular people who lack a certain cartoon coyote character. Blame it on the nurturing magic of entertainment.

Anyway, bundling everything of myself which broke apart upon crash-dummying into Ms. Tree – which, by the way, is an actual tree, okay – I crumple toward my front door.

Looking back at the evil-on-four-paws poking its head out of the newly remodeled entrance, a soft, delicate whistle calls Apocalypse back in.

43

FOLLOWING CHAPTER

The front porch. Pain. Hunger. Did I pay rent? Open door. Walk in. Pain. Feed the collection basket. Hunger. Hold it! I paid! Retrieve! Pain. Hunger. Kitchen. Mom in the kitchen cooking. More pain. No hunger. Why does she bother?

Her cooking tendencies serve as their own exterminators. Rats and roaches all understand raiding Mom's deathstock torture chamber supplies her with either the garnish or hors d'oeuvre folks rarely hunger for.

Yummm yummm.

Mulling over how I could convince Swydni to fashion an anti-Mom device that could rest on the stove, microwave and/or refrigerator, I stand at the kitchen entrance. I stand at the kitchen entrance directly behind my mother, wondering. Is she taking a plunger to the garbage disposal or fixing up one of her specialties?

Ahhh, idea.

"Mom? The sewer pipe busted in pop's den again."

Annnd gone! Grrrrreat!

Stepping to the sink where she was, I wonder what... no! Conquer the refrigerator instead! What she was doing should stay stationed in imagination.

Before Mom discovers my hoax, I best stock up on a few delectables and flee to the safe haven of my slumber sanctuary. Oh, what to choose? What to choose?

How about some cold cuts? And some hash browns? A pound of colby? Corn beef hash? A turkey? Half bird! And some cheese cake? And wash it all down with a diet coke!

Fascinating. These foods maintain a consistent normality at this pre-Mom stage. How it degenerates upon her contact haunts the dearly departed, as well as makes a few of them.

Something else more haunting: she fused an unidentifiable frying object on the windowsill. Nothing important, I just felt you had to know.

It may take a second or two before she hightails it back here after finding out Pops is dry. Or better yet, not horny nor "wasted." Before she does, I can practice. Practice a skill initially developed in hopes of parlaying it on a late night talk show, my stupid human trick later developed into a necessity.

Okay, set the food on the counter, open the cupboard and... There! Four pans, a pot and the electric sandwich maker in one swipe. Practice makes perfect. One rarely knows when a skill can come in handy. Anyway, necessity is the mother of inventions. That made no sense, but it offered the perfect segue for why I have to go.

Footsteps.

Yep. Time to go. Drop the metal stuff, scoop food – which proves my point – and vamoose. Uh oh. Forgot the bird. Retreat. Bite. Boogie.

"Richard!"

Damn! Caught at the sire escape.

"Haie Mah."

"Sit down and eat that food, Richard."

"Mahhhh."

Yes, one can whine and plea with a mouth full of turkey.

"Go on, Richard," waving me back in. "Sit!"

"P-tui! Mooom, I lost my appetite and, please, stop calling me Richard."

"We've gone through this already and already and already. Your name's Richard."

"Mooom."

"Your birth certificate says Richard. I call you Richard. You'll answer when I call you Richard and that's the end of the conversation, Richard!"

"People call me Dinky, Mom."

"Why, Richard? Are you small?"

"Mooom!"

"Well, Richard, if you wanted a nickname, use..."

"Richard, Mom! Call me Richard!"

"I thought so!" spoken like a true mom. "Now, what do you have there, Richard."

"I lost my appetite."

"Richard!!! Sit down!!!"

I sit.

"What's that? Turkey? About three and a third pounds? Cheese? Good stuff, too. Frozen hash browns? You like 'em crunchy, don't you, Richard?"

"Yes, Mom."

"Quiet, I'm working. What else? Assorted cold cuts? Slice of cheesecake? Two-liter bottle of diet cola? Corn beef hash, Richard? And... what? No bread? No bread? Okay, no bread."

Remember how I mentioned that there was another reason I seldom ate at home?

"That, Richard, will be $36.72 plus tip."

Now you know.

"Leave a real tip, too, Richard," slapping the check onto my forehead before she goes.

Oh, I could leave her something, all right.

Peripheral vision watches her leave. When she leaves, I do too. Upstairs, before heading out for real food. Quickly grooming – because priorities are priorities – I don my emergency clothes: a good cologne; a black cardigan with white trim; white mock turtleneck; black and white, glen plaid pants; black, patent leather slip-ons and creme purple socks with spacial, thin, black, vertical stripes that go up from the ankles.

Garbed properly, I feel... hunger. Thirty-six dollar pain. Hunger. Idea!

If I have to spend thirty plus on food, it should definitely be something I really want. And at this moment, I want food from...

"Mackey's!"

For the full effect of that scene change, you had to be here.

Mackey's. This place has ambiance. Mackey's is a ridiculous monstrosity posing as a fast food joint. The burgers suck, but the ambiance. Oh, the ambiance. Bumper-to-bumper female ambiance. People have met their future mates here. Last Saturday, alone, Mackey's housed a triple wedding. Unfortunately, the jerk owner, Mick Mackey, made the brides, who were his employees, clock on and prepare their own wedding menus.

Anyway, at the counter, I order a couple Mick Micks, a large Mackey fry and a super Mackey Mick pop. One warning, though, the food has so much grease, the buns have pimple seeds.

Time to find the proverbial empty seat.

Empty seat? Empty seat? Ah! Empty seat! With three other seats, filled to the gills with co-eds. I like co-eds. Especially when they teach co-education.

"Pardon me, ladies? May I sit here?"

"Sure."

What harmony.

Taking their generous, three-prong invitation, I sit. They stand. They leave.

Damn.

Preparing to drown my lonely sorrows in cholesterol, I let the crowd noise whisk me away.

Munch.

Yes. Burgers that explode tallow in your face.

Anyway, perhaps the murmurs of men and women can whisk me away. Maybe I can eavesdrop on a good conversation. Got one! Hard luck experience suggests it sounds like a man reading a newspaper article to someone else.

I get to eavesdrop a lot.

Go figure.

" ...and in Bullshead, Iowa, alcoholic Preston Bartholomew stumbled into a pasture and passed out. Apparently, the ninety-plus-degree temperatures caused Bartholomew to sweat profusely and several cows mistook him for a salt lick. According to Preston, the strange, uncomfortable and multiple sensations aroused him. He went into shock at the overwhelming sight of tongues and nostrils. David Farmer, resident farmer, found Bartholomew and rushed him to the nearest hospital in Nebraska. There, Preston revived swearing never to eat beef again."

"Amazing," the reading voice balks. "It's freaking amazing how these stupid things always happen to the other guy."

"What?!!! Who said those words?!!!"

My line of vision, somehow, rises above seat level.

"Who said those words?!!!"

The Other Guy. Merely thinking it can close my head for repairs and my body reacts. When the maintenance crew mends the grey matter, I find myself in predicaments tailor-made for sheer humiliation.

I liked eating lunch here. It typified my life. Mackey's seats a predominately small town of women. At four in the afternoon even, the only seats empty are the three those co-eds left me.

A worse-case scenario pops up when a loud, large crowd of people hushes, focusing its entire intuitiveness on one focal point.

Me.

Mayonnaise.

Yeah. Get out of this mess using some hokey excuse, ask a hokey question and cry when alone.

"Where, uh, do they keep the mayonnaise here? Anyone?"

They stare. How long will they stare?

A long time. A very long time.

Finally and fortunately, a totally out of whack Mack Employee comes within arms reach. I, and apparently he, have no idea what he pretends to perform. He does offer distraction. I grab him.

"Excuse me," whispering, "your condiments?"

"Aw, man," unwhispering, "I can't sell stuff off my person, court order, n'all. Here," handing me four quarters, "hook yourself up in the restroom."

"Huh?"

"Condiments? You want condiments? In the restroom. You're in luck, too. I put in some ribbed ones yesterday."

Could he tweak his volume control up another twenty decibels? Why let anyone in Carlisle miss out on this confab?

"Make sure you go in the right restroom, dude. Ain't no tellin' what four coins'll getcha in the skirts' room."

Look left. Look right. Look at him. React.

"Get away from me!!!"

This idiot removes all doubts of self-reproduction via hermaphrodital incest. Geez, what did that unbiodegradable dimwit distract me from, anyway?

Oh. The stares. Still got them. Maybe more. Do *my* ovaries work?! Maybe the exit sign should read "tixe" right about now.

Leaving the burger joint and making my way through the overcast and downtown foot traffic, the thought of how that place reflects so much befitting and immaterially haunting represents the totality of me via ying/yang-type situations. Go ahead and digest that thought while I take care of something.

"Excuse me, elderly person. May I help you across the street?"

"Who're you, >>whoomp<<, callin' elderly, >>whoomp<<, ya coot? Let me be."

"You use your umbrella quite well, lady. You invented hockey, right?"

"Let, >>whoomp<<, me be."

I do. She hobbles across the street. Her would-be assistant limps in the extreme opposite direction.

Anyway, that restaurant's conflicting dichotomies – harboring on multi-levels of near inconsequential sum and substance – illustrate the true representation of what sets Dinky apart, yet almost not apart, from Joe Average. Do you follow?

Far beyond supplying the oily nourishment, which exceeds Mom's standards, the place afforded more. Yingly speaking, I want female companionship... hard. I want to get busy, dizzy and squizzy [fictitious word meaning sex].

I go on record as admitting virginity. This lists as the underlying main plot. Not the virginity itself, but ridding myself of it.

About time, you ask? Why admit it now, so freely, you ask? Why not now, I ask!

Few things happen with consideration to calendars and convenience. Women, periodically, understand one and the other intrinsically. Besides, one's first sex is the main plot in almost everybody's life. Whether you admit it or not, whether it underlies your intended actions or not, sex does more than sell.

In the similar fashion of being at the restaurant, walking these streets bares the bofu of babes my pristine prays to party with.

Twenty-two years. No "private" action. I detect your thoughts.

Gross.

Yangly speaking, I want female companionship. For the untuned, that means I simply want a companion who happens to be female. For the in-tuned impaired... go to bed!

The sidewalks escalate under me. City blocks after city blocks circle from the strolling future to the sauntering past. Where am I going? What am I walking from?

This foot journey has shown too many examples of how fashions give women the chance to exposé. I see it, but I do not feel it. If I felt it, Conscience would wake up. Not good, because I really hate thinking about baseball scores.

It does prove a point, though. I want female companionship.

Swinging by Pops' old stomping grounds changes the scenery drastically. He hung his helmet in these parts. The stadium seems to radiate its aggression from the playing field outward onto the adjacent neighborhoods. Carlisle is a growing city, and just like any growing entity, it must nourish on something.

The benefits of poverty. Another topic for another circumstance.

Borrowing a touch from that topic attributes to my current situation. The more something grows, the more it feeds. The more something thrives, the more it weighs upon its support. If the feeder and the supporter are one, the equal-but-opposite theory exponentiates.

Before me represents an excellent example: a basketball court. More precisely, "Twenty-four-o-five."

Contrary to popular opinion, the roundball domain of the inner city seldom copies a warm hockey game: where there was a fight and a game broke out. Discrediting another rumor, the blacktops yield more than flashy, run-n-gun parodies of the professional league. Granted, it is not a corporate boardroom discussion in silk shorts, but those execs really mix it up, too.

Some of basketball's greatests are chiseled from the raw material finessing, powder passing and skywalking on concrete courts like this one. If books had far more than forty lines of resolution, you could watch, too.

Sorry.

I find a position just off the court and just off the street. Twenty-four-o-five uses traffic as a boundary line. If you get hit by a car, you were out of bounds.

What the...? Did I mention a warm hockey game? Well, there go two men in their eternal face-off:

Eugene and Lorenzo.

Nothing save anger comes between the rockhead and the hardass. Who started this encounter is anybody's guess. They seldom require a reason, anyway. Mix a contact sport with aggression, sweat, the win/loss coefficient and these two spices, and the flambé erupts naturally.

I met these guys in grade school. They battled over who saw me first. If possible, they would have tussled from the mothers' wombs. They transcend ultra competitiveness. Although, compared to their history, this current personality variance is tame.

They circle each other silently, like wolves. One day, their stupidity will engender fatality and/or worse. Mark my words.

Oh, you want to hear a kicker? They both own successful businesses. Again, go figure.

All right. Someone finally negotiated a cease-fire. Nonetheless, mark my words and let the games recommence.

As previously mentioned, some of basketball's greatest hail from war zones like Twenty-four-o-five. It also offers great video potential. My French horn laying down free-flowing background music, splashing alternating soothing-and-grooving licks. Devastating orchestra strikes syncopated with jams and slams like the one coming up.

Whoa!!! The way the last hombre dunked, he must be a flatfoot.
>>WooWooWoooo<<

The police? Okay, the joke lacked panache, but come on.

The over-populated basketball courts contribute meager attention to the cherried auto. Was it the joke after all?

The squad car door opens, spewing a phantom of a character. All men vaporize, including Eugene and Lorenzo. Who could intimidate so much tough?

Oh! Those guys' recognition abilities exceeded mine immensely.

The distance of a fast break separates me from the, uh, woman[?] who recently pulled over one of those tractor-trailer car carriers. She told the trucker he exceeded the limit and threatened a warning ticket. He copped an attitude.

Wrong move.

Rumor has it, this coppette informed him that since every car on the trailer exceeded the limit, she could issue a ticket for each one and force-feed them to him. He dared her. Anally speaking, the paper cuts kept him in intensive care for a month.

Rumor also has it officer she was a he. And he was German. A German, Olympic, heavy weight weight-lifter. After the competition years fettered by, s/he discovered its true femininity. This future policeperson opted for a sex change operation. In the middle of the procedure, the doctor suffered a major heart attack and keeled over on top of the reviving weight lifter. The attending staff rightfully panicked, saying the operation was a success.

S/he liked the results.

I have always found it difficult to swallow this rumor. Her accent says she has a French or Cajun background. Not German.

In actual reality, the behemoth in question dribbles toward me... without a ball.

"I noticed uh bulge on yur person. You carry'n a coun-cealed weap'n?"

>>Sigh<<

"Officer Hazel, we go through this every time you catch me out. My lone weapon is a .357 migraine. Not concealed!"

"Let me be da judj o' dat."

She will, too. Extending her long arms, she snares me, submerging my body in the folds of her... uniform.

"Ooooh. Why dey call you Dinky? Cannah prove it by me."

The only thing I want to prove by her is the secret release valve for her airbag body. This incident reminds me of a Newton theory about an object's gravitational pull being proportional to its mass.

Hazel has a lot of pull!

"Where'r dem weap'ns?"

Since her breasts effectively function as earplugs, I merely wonder about her wondering about the whereabouts of my coun-cealed weapons.

She has Bayou ancestry and she poorly stabs at the English vernacular, but her Russian hands and Roman fingers are languages she has mastered. And her bulk keeps me slurped, therefore, immobilized.

Hold it! Do I hear a bullhorn?

>>Shhhhhmlock<<

"Eeeuuw."

She unsuctioned me. Wwwwhy?

>>Ba-YUUUUU-ga<<

The meter reader?!

"Jump in."

Her voice barely registers. It registers enough for me to do my best get-in-the-awesome-sportscar-like-James-Bond imitation. Making the suave leap, I catch Officer Hazel still back-peddling from the bullhorn scare.

A mating call? Maybe. Anyway, before letting the plush bucket seat envelop my tush, my knee visits the glove compartment. Advice: never go somewhere uninvited.

"Custom-made hardwood dash?"

"Good guess," my emancipator responds, still barely above an intimate whisper.

"Thank you." Oh, the pain! "Why did you save me?"

"Had to if I wanted you for myself."

Sur-prise!

"I recognized you a couple blocks up. You were quite engrossed by the police there."

"Hazel."

"Yeah. We're acquainted."

Before inquiring how, my hero shoots me a smile and a Q.

"Hungry?" she asks.

"Uhhh..." Mom, check, stares, condiments. "Yeah!"

"Good. My treat."

"No prob," thinking over what just happened. "Would you mind if I take care of something first?"

She nods. I 180 my body in the seat.

When Officer Hazel collects herself – a sight to behold – she turns her attention at her deserting dessert. I, in turn, offer her a nicely ripened raspberry.

Childish? So what.

"Does driving under a viaduct in a convertible after a downpour mean anything?" my saving grace inquires.

What a funny question.

"Sthould it?"

"No," she sighs. "I guess not."

"Cool," and the tongue stays extended.

>>Plink<<

"Aaaaaaaaaaaaaaaaaah!!! Maie tung!!! Maie tung!!!"

"I tried to warn you."

"Peave, boo sompin!"

She reaches for my tongue. No. Under it and...

"Ow!"

Thumps the semi-solid, burgundy substance off.

Pulling in my bruised licker, the residual taste compares favorably to Mom's goulash.

"You gonna be alright?"

"Sure. A box of tic tacs always remedies the situation."

She smiles. How adorable. Then it hits me: Here I am varooming down the boulevard, companioned by a majestic representation of womaninity with a sheer, satin voice, in her equally majestic automobile. Something good has and may again happen to me... after I buckle up.

Moments later, the engine has offered the only communication, purring as it does. Stereotypically speaking, men feel awkward during conversial lapses. We chauvinistically need to continue the dialog, no matter how trite.

Personally, I stay quiet and let her assume my discomfort, rather than speaking, which will reveal it and major mental density. Thankfully, she breaks the silence.

"Nice socks."

"Thanks."

Clothes. Whew.

"Very few clothiers carry socks with this shade."

"Where did you buy them?"

"A ladies' hosiery shop. 'Socks and Such.' I have an account there."

More engine purr. Instants move. Again, she comfortably furnishes the oral ice pick.

"Where do you want to eat?"

"It matters not. I bow to your selection."

"I'll store that info for future use."

She purrs louder than the engine. Probably has more horsepower, too. I think this conversation needs more conversing on my part.

"Sooo, your name is…?"

"Kismet."

"Kismet? As in... fate? Destiny?"

She removes her attention from the road and her hand from the gearshift. She turns to me, slides the back of her fingers along the side of my face until she gets to the neck. There, she slowly flips her hand, brushing my neck with her fingernails. She uses the print of her thumb to outline the ridges of my ear before cascading her hand along my side to my shoulder, where she gives a playful squeeze.

"Exactly!"

She may purr softer than her engine, but no doubts remain over who or what has more horsepower.

"And, ummm, where are we going, Kismet?"

She returns her attention to driving.

"Here."

What a voice! What a woman! What a... Hold up! What did she say?

>>Rrrrrrrrrrrrrrrrrrrrrrrrch<<

Whoa! The seatbelt! The seatbelt stopped me from experiencing the windshield in a bad way! Then it hits me again: I was saved from Officer Hazel by a good golly! This same golly wants me! And I just escaped window pain?

"I'm sorry. The brakes grab sometimes."

"Noooo prob! No prob at all! Where are we?"

"A quaint little diner."

A glance at the marquee shows the name. "A Quaint Little Diner." How quaint.

"This place suitable, Dinky?"

"Yeah. Sure. Heeey! How do you know my name?"

"Let's talk inside."

Inside it is. Inside a place quite quaint. In fact, a quite quiet, quaint place. A place where the entrance doubles as a break in the space/time continuum. The decor resembles Camelot on Mars. Regal, yet harsh. Ancient, yet teal.

My "date" smiles at me. Her parted lips, clearly exhibiting Photoshop-perfect enamel, ignite a cinder at my feet. The rising temperatures climb. Please, I really do not need Conscience.

"Are you uncomfortable, Dinky?"

"Why?! Should I be?"

A tug on my collar releases a smoke signal.

"I don't bite," she quips.

Is that good or bad news?

"Let's sit down and order. After a good seven-course and equally satisfying discourse, you'll be dandy."

She may have a point. And with that, we seat ourselves.

"Okay, Kismet... talk."

"About what?"

"Yourself, your job, your... no! How did you know my name?"

"I know a lot about you, Richard."

My knees are sweating. This infernal gurgle is going to get my groin.

"Uhhhhhh, Kismet! H-h-how do you know so much?"

"My job."

Her voice.

"At the power company?"

"Yes. You know about "Big Brother," right?

"Sure."

"We energize him."

"Which means...?"

"Which means that if you invite me over for dinner, the only thing your mother better use in the kitchen is the telephone to order pizza and your father wears a waterproof suit."

Help!

"You're blushing. Sort of hard for someone of your pigmentation designation, isn't it?"

"Yeah. Yeah, of course. The food here is too spicy for me."

"We haven't ordered."

"Yeah. Right. Say, tell me about..."

"Russell?"

"You read minds, too?!"

"It's a woman thing."

"What antacids does this place serve?"

"I've upset you. I'm sorry, Dinky."

She reaches across the table and cups my hand. Uh oh. Conscience is now awake.

Yo, dude. What have you been trying to hide from me?

"Nothing! Shut up!"

"I said I'm sorry."

"No, Kismet, not you. My consc– My congestion flared up. Sometimes, talking to it like a... person helps calm me down. Heh heh. Call me weird."

Silence. Did she buy it?

"Okay, you're weird. My kind of weird."

She brings up her other hand and cups my other hand. My head bumps under the table.

Forget I wrote that.

"I'm sorry, Dinky. The last thing I wanted was to make you uncomfortable. In fact, I want just the opposite. I want you."

55

My hairline is liquidating.

"I'm being too forward, aren't I?"

"Huh? No. Puh-leeze."

She continues to hold my hands. Holding hands is a major desire. My wish. My joy. Kismet represents much more than a plot thickener. And all I have to do is say the word.

Come on, buddy. Let me say the word.

A hard pelvic thrust into the table quiets Conscience. It hurt him more than it did me. Actually, it hurt me as much as it did me, but it worked.

When the pain de-glaucomas, her demeanor fades into focus. At this moment and ever since the time I first laid eyes on her in my special window, Kismet represents everything I do and will hold dear.

But this is too much too soon.

"Kismet... darling... ummm... I think I should go."

Her wounded puppy expression begs me to stay. The waitress approaches.

I wipe her tear, kiss it off my knuckle, pause, then leave. While forsaking her, I hear Kismet's chair skid backwards.

Mentally begging her to stay as I unstay, the chair quiets. Somehow, something tells me that tele-pleading acted not as her stop sign.

Somehow something tells me what I heard the waitress murmur did:

"Let him go. If he's yours, he'll be so soon enough."

What was that suppose to mean?

Putting the quaint diner and the encounter behind me leaves me back on the streets in a vaguely familiar neighborhood. Living here all my life, Carlisle should have very few locational coverts.

>>Sigh<<

Why did I leave?

Yeah! Why did we leave???

No, not now.

No, tell me! Why did we leave? And another thing: you slam me against anything inorganic again and our bladder spits!

Conscience goes on and on while synchro-chunks pass us by as I make our way. Eventually, commonplace sets in. Not close to home, but a common place nonetheless.

I should have stayed.

I should also memorize a bus schedule. There are people who commit bus schedules to memory. They look like people who commit bus schedules to memory. For fun, they probably read phonebooks.

What a dumb hobby.

>>WooWooWoooo<<

Recreation note: commit bus schedules to memory.

"Awight, pull yo' butt ova to de curb. You ain't gettin' 'way dis time."

She – as in, "who else" – stops and gets out of her car. The air shocks inhale. Deeply. She wallows around the vehicle with a really long submarine sandwich in her grips and waddles toward me.

"Assume de poe-sition. Put yur hands up on de roo'."

"'De roo'?'" getting defensive. "What, per chance, is a 'de roo'?'"

"Don'cha be funny on me."

"First of all, officer, I want nothing of me on you and second, what is a 'de roo'?'"

She quickly grabs my wrists. The big woman can really move. Expecting handcuffs, she instead raises my arms and, >>ka-THOOM<<, gently places my hands on the roof of the squadcar.

"Dat's de roo'."

"Ow. I understand."

"Good. Now, we kin do uh strip-search fo' dem weap'ns."

Still assuming the position on de roo', I attempt a protest.

"You will not," >>wap<<, "deface my person," >>wap<<, "in such a manner," >>wap<<, "especially during rush hour," >>wap<<, "and stop slapping my head with that sandwich!!!"

"You ready fo' dis search?"

"No! >>Wap<< Can I come off this car?!"

>>Wap<<

"Of course, you know, this is police brutality."

>>Wap<< >>Wap<< >>Wap<< >>Wap<< >>Wap<< >>Wap<< >>Wap<< >>Wap<< >>Wap<< >>Wap<< >>Wap<< >>Wap<<

"Okay!!! Okay!!! Do the search!!!"

She sheaths her sub, wraps her mitts around me from behind and rips off my shirt. Thank goodness for snaps, specially designed for her type of carnage. Anyway, I feel her bilingual paws shimmy up my bare front. Up my stomach. To my chest, where she...

"Ow."

Pinches my pecs.

"Duz dat excite you, pooh bear?"

"No, grizzly. Not even close."

"Well, let'zee wha' fun I kin raize, >>rrrrip<<, below de belt."

Yep. These pants have snaps, too.

Hey! Heeey! Tell her to wash those mitts!

"Crawfish creole! Whut kinna streaks are dem on yur boxers?!"

"Those "stripes" are man-made."

"Ah, mon ami," she burps, "man made by you!"

"These stripes go horizontal, whoa-man! Step off and read!"

"So long's it ain't Braille," unwhisperingly whispering. "Don't go 'way."

I maintain my drapedness while Conscience complains about hygiene. Officer Hazel steps back as instructed. Each tread she takes makes me wonder how Dr. Scholl implanted heavy-duty struts in her shoes.

"'One Way?' Yur boxers say, 'One Way?'"

"Yeah," copping an attitude at this point. "Take the hint!"

Wrong move.

She closes the distance between us incredibly fast, places one hand on my right shoulder, crunches my street sign with the other and vaults me over her car. Doing a double somersault out of the pike position, my concrete splash pushes out enough air to vacuum-seal me upon landing. Face up. Officer Hazel then woddles around her squad car, kneels between my often-spreaded legs and seizes my undivided attention.

"How 'bout we search fo' dem coun-cealed weap'ns again? Cough!"

MIDDLE CHAPTER

She kept my socks! The pseudo-woman kept my socks! Of course, why not collect a souvenir of today's muddle on Main Street during rush hour? I guess I should be thankful she gave me back that which separated my au naturale from the leering public.

Nonetheless, I made it home and to the front porch. As a kid, this pouch served as my "safe base" whenever the neighborhood tykes played traditional games like baseball bat tag and kick the buckethead. Contemporarily speaking, this porch functions as my intermission between civic and domestic tribulations.

Reaching for the doorknob, I try to recall if I paid the rent. I walk inside.

"Surprise!!!"

Why is there a crowd of people in my house?

"Awwww!"

Okey dokey. They are *not* here for me! Why is there a crowd of people in my house?

Hmmm. A crowd of people yelling surprise. A crowd of people now deflated by my presence. Should this remind me what importance today carries?

Nope. Not even close. Who are these people and why are they – pausing to check the address out front – in my house?

Convinced this place serves as my residence, I scan the crowd. Two factions simultaneously pierce separate senses. Visually: Russell. But the nostrils swell, picking up a foreign entity at this address: Good food! Lots of it!

A "Wuts up, Russell," believably vents forth. The cultivating crowd noise practically drowns everything including itself and my voice. It also explains why Russell looks like he stars in one of those silent movies as he motions me to turn around. After I finish eating, he can tell me what he wanted. First, though, the food.

Preparing to brave the crowd, I step into the house. Before step one lands on step one, my surroundings start to change drastically. Sideways.

A quick glance at my friend shows him shrugging his shoulders before everything becomes a blur. Sideways.

Wind whistles in my ears and a touch of whiplash develops. A hypothesis suggests something snatched me. At the conclusion of my trip, the "upset" tour guide stands revealed.

"Pops," I peep. "Long time, no visit. How are you?"

"Don't talk down at me, boy," he grumbles.

I would oblige him had he not jacked me.

"Where's your present?"

Present? Present?

"Pooops! Did I forget your birthday? Here," still peeping, "take a tic tac and let me get back to you."

"Whaaat?!!!!"

Scar tissues protect my eardrums from his outcry. Swydni fashioned earplug earrings she wears at home for just such emergencies. Everybody else's unprotected balance center gets shredded. Since Pops never pays attention to public opinion, their appearance serves as no embarrassment to him. Just to me.

"It's your mother's birthday, boy. Where's her present?"

As I dangle, babbling in hopes something intelligible spews out, a speckle of spit jumps off my bottom lip and lands right on the tip of Pops' nose. He looks at it, looks up at me, growls, raises me to chandelier levels and...

"Oscar?"

Saved by the dingbell.

"Kath? Aww, baby, welcome home."

Amazing. Simply amazing. How can his moods instantly switch from crazed to suck-up?

"You set up another surprise party for me, honey?"

"Yeah, baby," he grovels. "Happy birthday."

Mom walks in and surveys her house. She pays no mind to husband and son in common ritual. Inspecting the gathering of wounded individuals, she spies something which sparks her ire.

"Who brought food into my house?"

"Came with the presents, baby."

Yes. He is groveling. Grovel, grovel, grovel.

"Oh," she calms. "I can handle that."

"Pops," trying to take advantage of his lighter attitude, "could you put me down?"

"Shut up, boy," snapping under his breath.

>>Kaff<< And what breath.

"Pops. Take a tic tac. I promise to get you another one. Gift wrapped, even."

"Oscar, honey? Where're my presents."

On cue, gifts of all shapes, sizes and colors bombard Mom, completely covering her standing body. Pops, hating to be left out and never releasing me, picks up a poorly wrapped microwave box and hurls it at her. Good shot, too. Since Mom now lies crumpled in the foyer after receiving Pops' endowment, it is a safe bet to assume he did chuck her a microwave.

"Throw your present at her, boy," returning his attention to me.

Reaching into my pocket, I pitch a handful of lint and smile gleefully.

"Uh uh," he nods. "It's not the thought that counts."

He pauses. I hear synaptic sparks. In these situations, the thing to remember is that no matter what, keep the body limp.

"You gave me an idear, boy." Looking over his shoulder, he orders, "somebody open'a door."

"Sure, Pops," Swydni happily offers.

I hope her silicon chip implants distort her head.

"Like you threw air, boy, I'mma throw an air-head."

"No, Pops! It was lint!"

Sis climbs over Mom and opens the door, revealing nature's haunting persona. The winds briskly whip foliage, moving them into animation. Branches resemble arms sweeping inward as if asking for something. Leaves rustle, creating noises not far from words. In fact, the big tree in the front yard acts like it motions to Pops.

"Oscar. Give him to me, Oscar. Give him to me."

This scenario, occurring during dusk, hardly helps keep my fears in check.

Pops steps over Mom and indulges the tree, which means...

"Whoa!"

The speed streaks return. Not sideways this time.

Sailing like a javelin over the porch means domestic tribulations cease and civic ones commence. The first one this evening comes right about
>>Wham<<

Hmmm?
>>Sthmack< >>Sthmack<<

Raw toothpicks. Maple-bark flavored. I just wish my face had its sensors back. Then I could tell if my mouth opened before the natural shrapnel inserted themselves between my teeth. Tribulation numbers one and two.

Oh, well. I could and should rest up a bit. Yeah. Why not rest up a bit? Rest up and build my strength before another tribulation. At least until the pain recedes.

"Ughhhhhhn."

Unwrapping myself from Ms. Tree, many moments later, the pavement welcomes me. And why not? We both know an all-evening pounding shall be a-happening today.

After a while – and a few cracks to break my father's back – the sidewalks tell me Pops has a point. Forgetting Mom's birthday lists way up there as a major no-no. His "reminders" do fit the crime, cohering with my normal vicissitudes.

It all makes me think. It really makes me think. It makes me think of growing up as a contact sport, it makes me think. It makes me think I have very few thoughts on the norm, it makes me think.

Growing up, a contact sport. Me, a contact magnet.

Putting this thought into proper perspective requires imagination, per se. A stadium with lights and fans screaming for macho mayhem. Imagine, if you will, television announcers of the National Dinky League:

"Howdy, pain fans and welcome to the NDL on ESDN. I'm Argo Thickneck, along with color commentator, Chad Plaid.

"It's a beautiful night here in Carlisle as the moon hangs majestically over Sundown Stadium. The weather? What else, but overcast at a comfortable 72 degrees.

"Tonight, an expected brutal battle between bitter arch rivals, the Motown Maulers and the host, Carlisle Cramps. Here to explore the history and future of tonight's broadcast is former all-NDLer, like me, Chad Plaid. Chad?"

"Tanx, Argo. For da past one-two-twee years, da Crwamps hauv enjoyed livin' up to deir title as da wimps ov da league. Against da Maulers, da Crwamps again expect anoder blowout weception, never see'n' da endzone until aftah da game, when they hafta mow da field. Da Crwamps are led by qwauterback Wichard Deankey, who leads da league in ambulance wides and expects at least one-two mo' twips tonight. Dat's the pudge match inna nutshell... back to you, Argo."

"Thanks, Chad. You know, you're proof positive Elmer Fudd and Arnold Swartzenegger could be one person."

"Dah. Tanx."

"Alright pain fans, let's play ball. Cramps captain, Deankey, trots toward the middle of the field as... as... everybody else looks up? What's up, Chad?"

"Da moon, Argo, for anoder moment or one-two."

"Huh? Oh! As, uh, previously announced, the moon hangs over Sundown Stadium. But now, the cosmic bungee cord don't wanna hold it no more. Obviously, everybody except Deankey notices the problem and scrambles from the stadium.

Quick! Somebody set up a split screen between the Cramp QB and the moon. Maybe we can get his reaction upon impact and boost our ratings. Yes! Perfect!

"Alright folks, we're here live
at the scene of a rare – soon
to be phenomenal – occasion.
This left side shows the moon
over Carlisle that won't be
over Carlisle in a moment.

"And the right side gives
America the in-your-face
angle on the man who'll
have the moon land on
him.

"Any second folks, the action
will... Holy cheap
cheerleaders! There it is!"

>>BerrrBOOOOOMMMMMMMMM<<

"What a spectacle! But we
seem to be having technical
difficulties with the Dinky
Cam."

>>Kershhhhhhhhhhh<<

"It appears the heavenly body
took out our camera man, too.
No biggie. Hopefully, we can
get a replay on Deankey's
reaction before the lunar
touchdown.

"Yes! That's it!
Obviously, the man had
no clue what's to fall on
him. There! Right there!
He notices the camera
man. How did he twist his
face into a question mark?

Did'cha see it? If we can
slowly backplay the...
tape... to... Freeze it! Let
me draw one and... Bingo!
Perfect match! Okay,
continue rolling. Deankey
has mere moments left
before..."

>>Kershhhhhhh<<

"The Sea of Tranquillity takes him out. Hey, Chad, you were
on the money about that ambulance ride."

"Dah."

"Uh huh, riiight. Anyway, as the moon trots off the field with a
blotched Deankey coming over the top, we'll wrap up our
broadcast of the NDL on ESDN. I'm Argo Thickneck. He's
Chad Plaid. And we return you to network reality with The
Other Guy. Ah-dee-osee."

Hi. Remember me? Dinky? As you realize, even my fantasy TV lacks immunity from Murphy's Law. It, too, bends into my actual continuance. The moon pebble in my shoe acts as proof positive.

So, I have a possible krypto-pellet in my odor eaters, Mom's birthday slipped my mind again, I smell like a tree doctor and the split page offered enough distraction for me to wonder somewhere I have never been. Not bad for thirty minutes. Maybe assessing these problems in reverse order may help eliminate them.

Yeah. Right. Where am I?

The long shadows, which come when the sun gives its final daily nod, hinder complete recognition. Primarily because as light strikes an obstacle, it renders all objects on the opposite of the light source from said obstacle lightless. It customarily extends discomfort toward any person within the near-void illumination. In other words, dark grows fears. Fears siphon awareness. Incomplete awareness obstructs the acknowledgement of the predicament I reside in.

Where am I?

"Mind some company?"

Although familiar, the voice animates the evening and my phobias.

"S-s-sure. Where are you?"

The confidence in that line will surely wart off any attackers.

"Over here, Dink."

Dink?

"Russell?"

He "appears," leaning against a building in an alley. A mysteriously prosaic alley.

"I've been waiting on you," he claims. "Fortunately, I passed the time chatting with a cute little redhead girl."

Redhead girl? Alley?

"Say, uhhh, Russell, how were you... waiting on me?"

"Don't worry about it. Just understand I'm here. Always your friend. Willing to help."

"Willing to help? How?! If you remember correctly, Mom got knocked out under everybody's present but mine!"

"Go get her one now. It'll satisfy her and calm your father."

"What do I get her?! Where do I shop?!"

"It's your mother. Didn't she drop some hints in the past few days?"

"Mmmmmaybe."

"Maybe? Don't you listen to her, Dink?"

"Mmmmmaybe."

"You're hopeless," he sighs.

"Popular opinion," I spoof. "And a thought just dawned on me, dude: where we can shop?"

"The mall."

"The mall?"

"Don't you dare tell me you don't know about it."

"Uhmmmmm."

"You're hopeless."

"I told you, my friend, popular opinion. Where is it?"

"A block over," pointing his head in our intended direction.

Embarking on more unaccustomed territories, Russell feigns his pre-conversational posture. Whenever silence permeates us, he stares straight ahead, unless an activity previously held his attention. It helps him focus during our customarily nonsensical chats.

Trying not to engage in one, something other than Mom's gift and Pops' rift plagues my faculty.

"Russell?"

"Yeah, Dink."

"Mind if I pose a Q?"

"You just did. Twice."

I hate that rattling sound I get when I shake my head, attempting to clear it.

"Can I ask another one?"

"You just did."

"Rus-sell!!!"

"Okay, Dink," he smirks, "go ahead."

"Your name?"

"That's the question?"

"Stop changing the subject."

"I didn't know we had one."

"Russell!" trying to suppress a migraine. "How did you get your name?!!"

A slight pause eases my tension. These conversations – lack of a better word – come nowhere near common tête-à-tête. Apparently, these dialogues have greater meaning. Either that or someone recently flaked me off of a prune danish.

"My name gives me originality," he finally metes. "The people out and around carrying one name changed theirs. Me? It's my birthright."

As previously mentioned, whenever the two of us talk, his head locks in the forward position, rarely moving, except for out of necessity. So, when he tilts his head and stares upward, it signals the arrival of something... different.

"Then, of course, there's..."

See? Might as well play along.

"Tell me, Russell."

"My cousin."

"Your cousin?" rapidly bantering.

"Watt."

"What?"

"Yeah."

"What? Hold it," allowing my brain to catch up with the exchange. "Can we start over here? You - have - a - cousin - named...?"

"Watt."

If looks could kill, divine intervention should resurrect him, so I can Louisville slug him, too.

"Are you going to tell me?!"

"I just did."

"What?"

"Right."

"Arrrrrrrrrrrrrrrrrrrrrrrrrrrrrrgghhh!!!"

I give up! Meanings or not, nobody deserves this. Walking away from my... associate, I try concentrating on the problems which put me in the street in the first place. Barely three steps later, Russell reaches out and grabs my shoulder.

How I long for super death vision.

"My cousin," he tranquilizes, "his name is Watt. W-a-t-t. My... um, mother understood how a person's name affects them, shapes their personality. My dub grants self-shapement."

"Cool. I understand." Well, not really, actually. "But your cousin? How did his name shape him?"

"He's a three-way."

I outright refuse to ask what, or watt, that means.

We resume the permeating silence, soon broken by my reaction as we cover the distance from our prior spot to...

"The Mall!"

Often, this place – actually named, "The Mall" – supplies backdrop to many festival occasions which later show up on "Film at Eleven." The prototype shopping complex of a growing, grown city, this entity gives testimony to the aggressiveness the community's founding fathers never fathomed.

A displaydial marketing kaleidoscope of merchandise engrosses this visitor in the similar fashion of a youth at an evening Independence Day celebration. The abundance of stores would further impound my attention if not for the multiple fireworks of femininity.

Boom. Boom. Boom. What a fine momma. Literally. Her baby could use some beauty hibernation, though. Or a zookeeper.

Homina, homina, homina. The pants on that blonde? Tight enough to have pours.

Ayyyyy! Liposuction alert! A herd of them in a shoe store. Poor clerk. Probably has a mock wife and two kids to boot.

What the...? An Asian with auburn hair? Looks natural, too. And those topless sandals. Makes me wonder what flavor those toe rings are.

"You're pathetic."

On that note, peripheral vision harshly gravitates my entire deliberation away from shorts to shorty. Although quotation marks never encompassed my thoughts, they must have encased my facial expressions.

"You, my friend, are a dog."

"Me, Russell? Dog? Arrruf!"

"You're pathetic," sighing of pity again. "This display towards females today is totally abominable."

"O-Okay, man," noticing his seriousness, "I apologize. Is this thing with females personal?"

"Nooo. No. No! I simply understand women. Better than you, it seems. There's no telling the benefits a better understanding could do for you."

Why is he blasting me?

"Let's get your mother's present, please."

Why is he blasting me?

Walking through the mall, I keep a poker face in case... oh, my good golly! Sharp eye-ricochet at Russell. Never noticed. Good. Speaking of good. Another good gooder golly. I feel a seething stare. Straighten up. Straighten up.

No! No! Please, no!

Heading my way, an oscillating pair of hips that leave a trail of bread chumps wherever they have been. What bodacious lines she has, very nicely smothered in red lace and lycra. Candy apple red, at that!

Uh oh.

"Hey, Russell. How you doing, man?"

"We talked about this," conjecturing a deep tone.

"Yes, we did."

"What's up on the groping, then? Your saliva wants to peep that woman, too?"

"Huh? Wh-what woman?"

"Dink," he sighs. "The woman with the six inch heels."

Something about the way he said "six inch heels."

"What woman with six inch heels?"

"The same one in the candy apple red almost-a-dress."

Why is he talking like I should know what he means? Six inch heels? Candy apple red?

"All you need now is a ventilation grate."

Ventilation grate?

"Forget it."

"Forget what?!"

"I said, forget it!"

"Cool. I can do that."

"We're here."

"And where is here, Russell? Hold on. What is this? Cyd... Syd... Sid...?"

"It's pronounced, "side orders." They advertise on "The Rose" all the time."

"Cy'd Orders? The Rose?"

"Cy'd Orders, you're standing in front of. The Rose, the number one station in town."

"Gas?"

"Radio."

"The Rose?"

"WROZ. Forget it. Just catch the movie when it comes out."

[Author's note: that was a beautifully shameless plug for a totally different project.]

"Russell? Did you hear something?"

"No, what?"

"A voice?"

"Yes, I did."

"Really?!"

"Sure. We're in a mall full of people. Chances are a couple of them might say something, Dink."

"No. I mean... forget it! Just forget it! I know I heard it!"

"Heard what?"

"Stop patronizing me, Russell!"

"Dink. I'm sure you heard someone. If he/she/it really wanted your attention, they'd get it. But for now, you need to check out what Cy'd Orders has for your mother."

"I hate you. You know that, right?"

"That's what friends are for."

And into the place we walk.

It takes no time to realize Cy'd Orders epitomizes a typical example of Commercialism 'R' Us. The redundancy of the last statement reinforces the fact. This place first offers the glass storefront which gives window shoppers a lot to shop. It also goes far as to shelve an assortment of chocolate-covered pet food for gerbils, birds, boa constrictors, etc. The only thing this store appears to lack is modesty. This "Cy" character probably hails from Texas, which the size of Cy'd Orders, alone, has me to guess. Being as large as the major department stores, Cy'd Orders probably anchors the mall, too.

"Dink, this place has an abundance of respectable presents. Stay clear of the novelty sections."

"Of course, Russell. Nothing but the best for my momma."

No sooner than uttering what Mom deserves, something catches my attention, attracting my person.

"Dink?! Where are you going?!"

"I saw something."

"Not over there!"

"Why not?" tossing the Q back while I beeline to my conquest.

69

"You're heading towards a novelty section."

I ignore him, speeding to the perfect present. Yes!

"Put it down, Dink!"

Did he say something?

Picking up a sure-fire present for anyone with my parents' quirks would admire... Hold it! Who would have their quirks? The parents of another Other Guy?

Anyway, instructions? Where are the...

"Ah! Instructions: Add water. She can handle this."

"Dink, don't!"

"Why?"

"Look at it," he pauses. "What is it?"

"Self-contained, plastic aquarium with life-like, imitation plastic fish."

"Why even think about getting her that?!"

"You told me Mom contrivedly dropped some hints in the past few days."

"So?"

"Sooo, she mentioned plastic and fish in the same sentence just last week."

"Were you honestly paying attention to her?"

"Should I have?"

"You're pathetic, Dink."

"Common opinion, my friend. Common opinion. Point me to the register. Never mind. I see the signs."

I walk past my friend, proud of my selection for Mom. Something tells me that between Russell and me, the proud is mine alone.

"You're not gonna give her fake plastic, are you?"

Sign me up for a psychic network.

"The plastic is as real as my intentions. If you want me to give her something else, you pay for it."

I glance back at him, noticing my trailing compadre reach for his wallet.

"No!!! My mommy! My money! My present!"

The windy words physically stopped him. Imagine what they did to his hair. When Himacane Dinky subsides, he simply proposes:

"Make sure it's completely assembled."

"Good idea," lowering the enthusiasm. "Using water may entice her to boil it."

"The fish?"

"The whole thing."

We make our way to the cashier, or a reasonable facsimile, thereof. It never fails. Whenever you want to leave a shopping experience in a hurry, the outlet-powers-that-be want just the opposite. In a store this size, is it too hard to expect more than two cashiers on duty?

Half an hour later, I see the cash register. Fifteen quicker customers stand ahead of me, but I see the cash register.

Ten minutes later, I spot the cashier.

Whoa. Whoa. Whoa! I thought my genitors were bad! Who bumped nuptials to incept that clerk?

Eleven transactions later put us face-to-face. Face-to-face with an abnormality. A paradox. An incongruity. A mess.

An African-American geek.

Picture the nerdiest, nerder nerd nerdestly envisaged, stereotypically depicted from the Caucasian persuasion, perhaps? You got it? Now, color him with a pigmentation crayon.

Did you "whoa," too?

Buck teeth, overbite, horn-rimmed glasses held together with masking tape, of course, two pocket protectors and a mini calculator rolled up in his sleeve like a pack of cigarettes. Probably a renegade accountant.

And his clothes. Oh, why does he hurt me? Orange and brown striped shirt. Earth green, double-knit, reversible slacks. And white socks, which lay exposed because the bottom of his pants and his ankles have never met.

This hurts. This hurts bad.

"Hi. I'm Cy Jr."

No surprise there. Was not expecting him to be nasal, though.

"Was your shopping experience satisfactory, sir?"

Wow, his teeth! Either Bugs Bunny lives in his petrified family tree or those animal-to-human transplants have gone too far. I also noticed that his breath smells empty. His cologne more than makes up for it, though.

"Your cologne, Cy Jr...?"

"Hai Karate and Stri-dex. My body gets zitty sometimes."

Too easy.

"What's your name?"

"People call me Dinky."

"Sex?"

"With you, Cy Jr.? Puh–"

"That's not what I meant. Don't worry, you'll catch it next week."

I think... I think I lost the offensive.

"What's this?" inspecting my intended purchase. "Plastic fish???"

"For my mother."

"You're kidding."

"No. Why?"

"Dinky?"

"What?!"

"Not sex. Thought supplies your name."

I think this nerd is funning me. The laughing line of customers behind me could be the give-a-way.

"You might understand next month... Dinky, is it?"

"You have a problem with my name, Jr.?

"Cy Jr. and the problem's yours."

The mass of mirth increases, which means the nerdy Abscess Jujitsu Jr. razzes me despite my non-understanding. I grab the present, flip him two twenties and leave him AND the smiling Russell behind.

Would Jr. let me leave in peace?

"A tip?"

No.

"Hey, Dinky, I'd'a ribbed you for free. Wanna receipt?"

Outside the store, totally embarrassed and quickly heading toward the mall exit, I hear my confidant chuckling behind me.

"You could have helped."

"You should have listened to me in the first place."

"Well..."

"I saw lint in the next aisle."

"Shut up, man! My problem was Jr., not the present!"

"Cy Jr., you mean."

The re-fueling anger temporarily locks my jaws. My race pace for the exit goes pacier. Every few steps, a poorly refrained snicker escapes my trailing friend. His last one, and the source of them, prompts me to pose a Q. It does not, however, slow my departure from this suddenly huge-er shopping complex.

"Russell, what is the female equivalent of a nerd?"

"You're not a nerd, Dink."

"Not me! Jerk Jr.!"

More poorly refrained snickers.

"A the Q, please!"

"What Q?"

"The female equivalent of a nerd?"

"A female nerd."

"No, I mean... dammit!"

Almost at the exit.

"What is a... female pocket protector?"

"An underwire bra with six hooks."

He knew that?

"You knew that?"

"That wasn't me, Dink, and..."

>>ch-pwam<<

"That door says 'pull.' You alright?"

"Uh, yeah. Ummm... why are you so tall?"

"Because you're laid out, Dinky."

Dinky? Dinky? He never calls me Dinky.

"Help me get him up, please, Russell."

Bending down, they grab my arms, bringing me up. They?

"A friend of yours, Dink?"

"As soon as my eyes become mostly sunny, we both will know."

"It's me, silly. Kismet. I'm sorry you misread the door, but your accident let me catch you... and Russell."

"I take it you two have met before?"

"Once," they synch.

Weird.

Despite my attempts to visually keep my supports at two people, I notice them stare each other down while keeping me propped.

"Dink, I believe Ms. Kirk cares for your company."

"Who?"

"Kismet. Kismet Kirk. You didn't... never mind. Listen, I gotta take care of something. I'll leave you folks to find your fun."

"Russell? Russell?!"

My voice loudens as he increases our distance.

"Russell, why are you leaving me?!"

"You're in good hands, my friend," he tosses back. "Or at least you will be."

Wonderful.

"I told you, Dinky, I don't bite."

Small consolation.

"C'mon," she tugs.

"Where?"

"Where you definitely need to be."

"And that is?"

"Church. Evening services."

"Church? Big building with a cross on top?"

"C'mooon."

She drags me outside to her car, parked in the front row of the lot. Now, I can squeeze my knowledge of cars into a croissant and have enough room for half a cow to make a sandwich. But I do know red. I do know convertible. I do know awesome.

"You really need this, Dinky."

"The car? I agree."

"No, silly."

"Oh. You mean evening services. Hey, Kismet, normally church and I get together a lot, but I..."

"Wanna drive?"

"After you, my dear."

Before tossing me the keys, she presses a button on the key chain. The car barks.

"Unlocks the doors?"

"Unlocks the doors."

I open my door, toss my butt inside and... should I be a gentleman?

"Don't bother, Dinky. I can let myself in."

Whoa! Forgot about her woman thing. Anyway, I fire up the engine while searching for the "top down" button.

73

"Above the radio. Third button to the left."

Her woman thing is making me nervous.

"I'll stop."

Thank you.

"You're welcome."

Stare. Look away. Stare again. Stare again, hard.

She leans over and kisses me on the lips. Was I thinking about something?

"Put the car in gear," she purrs mere inches away.

Yeah! That was it! I check oncoming traffic annnnd boogie!

"Kismet, where are we going?"

"Evening services."

"Where? What church?"

"Just drive."

Nuff said.

I weave in and out of traffic before emerging from the mall parking lot. Stopping at the light, I get the notion this car had a prior life as a dragster.

"You ever push a vehicle like this before?"

"No, ma'am."

"Then take the highway and open it up."

"Heh. No prob."

Green light. Onramp. Zoom!

Many, many highway miles later, 95 red lines third gear. Kicking it into forth, I suddenly remember we had a destination. My companion has silently watched me enjoy her mobile all this time. But we had a destination.

"Kismet?"

"Turn here."

Off-ramp. Slow. Down shift. Stop sign.

"Turn right and open it up again."

Turn onto narrow roadway. Gas. Shift. Much gas. Shift. Much more gas. Shift. Get funky gas.

"Stop here, Dinky."

"Here?"

"Here."

"Invisible church?"

"No. Stop."

Brake. Slow. Stop. Pan.

"You have a cornfield congregation, Kismet?"

"I like your sense of humor."

"Thanks. Annnd we are... where?!"

"Where the sun calls it a day."

Uh huh.

"Rain, snow, drought, I come out here and give thanks. Out yonder on that mound," she points, "the sun gives me the Lord's message."

"I bet he gives a blistering sermon."

"That's not funny."

"Sorry," lowering my head in embarrassment. She raises it, placing to fingers under my chin.

"I'm sorry."

I want her! Not sexually... well, yeah, sexually. Not at this moment, though. Well... change subject.

"Do we need Bibles, Kiz?"

"The Word's in here," touching my chest. "Answering your question: Faith is a muscle. The Bible trains it. A membership at God's Gym pumps it up, because..."

"Because the more you use it the bigger it becomes."

"Right. And if you don't use it, you lose it."

We leave the car and roam the plains. Walking about two... three hundred yards, I take advantage of the conversational lull to do the unthinkable: appreciate where I am.

Mother Nature? Our Father? Whoever has that grand paint brush did it right. More colors than a paint store. More shapes than an advance geometry class.

Speaking of shapes...

"Dinky? The Lord grants us all serenity, strength and wisdom. You'll always have them here," touching my chest again, "and here," my forehead.

She stops and pauses, glancing toward the heavens.

"The sun's about right. Ready?"

"Ready? Ready for what?"

"For prayer."

Prayer. Dinky Definition: set alarm clock to Amen.

"If you care to join me, close your eyes, bow your head, open yourself up and stay awake. I didn't read your mind; I just know you."

Okay, no prob. Close my eyes and stay awake. Stay awake. Stay awake. Z... no. Stay awake. Stay awake. Zzz... no! Zzzzz... no!! Zzzzzzzzz. Ah, zzzzzzzzzzz z z z zzzzzzzzzzz zzzzzzzzzzzzzzzzzzzzzzzzzzzzzzzzzzzzzzzzzzz.

Zzzzzzzzzzzzzzzzzzzzzzzzzzzzzzzzzzzzzzzzzzzzzzzzzzzzzzzzzzzzzzzzzzzzzzzzzzzzzz. Zzzzzz. Zzzzzzzzzz. Zzzz. Zzzzzzzzzzzzzzzzzzzz zzzzzzzzzzzzzzzzzzzzzzzzzzzzzz. Zzzzzzzzzzzzzzzzzzzz zzzzzzzzzzzzzzzzzzzzzzzzzzzzzzzzzzzzzzz zzzzzzzzz zzzz zz zzzzzzz.

"Amen."

"Hell-o!"

"You fell asleep, didn't you?"

"Me? Puh-leeze. Naw, the Big Guy and I connected fiber-optically."

She simply smiles, stands and motions me to follow.

"Where to now?"

"My place."

"Y-y-your place?"

"Don't worry, I don't bite. Not unless you beg me to."

Momma.

We get in her car. She gets under the wheel. I get under the proverbial rock.

"We're here."

What? When did the car move? Or did the city move? When did the top come up? My nerves. Oh, my nerves.

"Dinky, we're here."

I do another area pan. We seem to be... in the garage of her apartment complex, I assume? A neon sign reads, "A Quaint Domicile." How quaint. Oh, my nerves.

"C'monnnn."

We climb out and head across the parking garage. She points her key chain behind her. The car barks.

All of the sudden, the escorting Kismet reminds me of Apocalypse. They both want the same piece of Dinky Estates. Question is, will she foreclose like the dog wants to?

Shortly thereafter, in the elevator, she reaches for my hand, squeezing it gently. Might as well have been my stomach.

The >>bink<< >>bink<< which signify a passing floor are on beat with the hip hop musac. Nice touch.

No more bink. No wonder. Top floor. Who is this woman?

The doors slide apart. She departs, tugging me to follow. A weird relevance nearly overwhelms me. With each step, my tension eases. I realize I want this. My chest swells and not because of the usual almost-lost-my-virginity asthma attack. I feel good for once. This seems more right the more we range.

This walk down the hall, though, takes longer than the drive here. Much longer.

Finally, at her door, she unlocks it. My nerves prevent me from paying attention to what lock system it is. My nerves or my ease? Right now, it is very hard to split the difference.

So much for relevance. We go inside.

I enter her apartment after her, puppy-dogging at her heels all the way to the leather couch. Yap. She stops, spins and places her hand on my chest, halting me in one very smooth motion.

"Do you mind of I slip into something more comfortable?"

"Ah. No."

"Stay there," she puckers vixenously.

She pecks and heads away. On her way out of the room, Kismet walks past a rather big television. She points her key chain at it. It barks before fading on.

As the tele gains total visualization, I recline to inspect, peruse and probe her alcove. Nice place.

"Dinkyyyyyyyyyyyyy."

I spin toward the tune. Use your imagination to imagine what she has on.

No clue? Bingo!

"You like, sir?"

"Yap."

"It's the most comfortable thing I couldn't find."

"Happy birthday to me."

Before coming out of the shadowy hall, she reaches for what is inevitably an obscured switch, thus dimming the lights. The shadows appreciated that move, because they stay on her longer. I cannot see her entire body, but I see her body. More than enough.

She sways around the couch and onto me. My, is it hot all of the sudden?

"Don't worry, mister. I'll lead."

She takes my hand and serves me the sweetest French pastry kiss. Truly like nothing I have ever encountered, whether in the movies, on TV or as a peeping tom. Surely, nothing I personally experienced comes close.

This woman personifies smooth. Not "Colt 45" smooth, either, Billy Dee. Sssmmmmooooooooth-a!

Her hands leave mine, glide to my back and travel south. Once crossing the border into Rearendo City, Mexico, she squeezes. I react.

"Nice," she breathes. "Tongued your tonsils there. Had I deduced such a reaction, I would have crossed these hot buns sooner."

Things are happening too fast. Waaay too fast!

Whenever Pops described personal situations with strange similarity, he would mannishly expound, "never look a gift whore in the mouth."

I hope he meant horse, otherwise somebody will chafe really bad. Why am I thinking of Pops, anyway?

For what seems like forever, I encounter lips. Lips, lips and more lips [above the chin, thank you]. Lips, lips and...

Where did the floor go?! I remember braving it when I got here! Where is it?!

My toes tap out, searching, probing for that... that... that big flat thing that perpendics gravity. The feety digits report back with no news.

I break the embrace to notice I went horizontal. On the couch. With her on top. Things are happening way too fast!

"Kismet, >>smwauw<<, Kismet, I, mmmmm, I have to go."

"What, baby?"

"I, mmmm, have to go."

"That's another feeling you have down there."

She lost me. My pause lets her resume the fondle assault.

"Kismet," lifting her soft supples off me, "I have to go."

She finally understands. Almost.

"Please. Not now."

"I hate to leave you hanging, again, and leave you hanging, but I really, really have to go.

A silent tear drops onto my cheek.

Still upholding her, I slime off the couch, placing her where I was. How did she position me there? Why I am putting HER there?!!

"Please, forgive me."

Unvoiced, her body speaks volumes.

Her blinds allowed the city's night lights to splash her toes, the convenient curves of her legs and her hip, streaking to a halt on the upswoop of her left breast. A beautiful breast, which shadows the sensitivity of her right. No shadow falls, though, upon her beautiful face, her tears, her outreached hand.

"Hold me," it says. "Let me bring you back."

Conscience. Conscience would let you hold it. Let you bring us back. Where is Conscience?

She weeps as the door closes behind me. What have I done? What have I done?

In the elevator, my heart clamors, thundering over the binks. Near the top of this newly christened dumbwaiter, the floor indicators flash the passing tier and how far I descend from the top. From the top.

What have I done?

The last bink rings loud. Street level. My heart goes basement. Sub-level thirty.

Again, nightfall in Carlisle finds me pounding pavement in dilemma. What else could go wrong?

Alright, Kismet! Get ready to rummmmmmmblllllle! Kismet? Kismet?

"Conscience?"

*Hey dude, we can talk about your spectacular powers of recognition later, *after* we take a ride with lady luck. Where is she?*

"At home."

At home? Where are we?

"We left."

WE WHAT?!!!!!!!!?!!!!!!!?!!!!!!?!!!!!?!!!!?!!!?!!?!?

A screaming Conscience. A painful first.

What! Have! You! DONE?!!

"Keep it down, will you?"

I want to keep it up! It is my job, remember! A job among at least one other job we should be involved with right now!

"Where were you when things started?"

I put you on cruise control. Figured you could handle it.

"Put me on what!?!!!"

I had some unfinished business.

78

"Like what?"

How bad do you want to know?

Silence.

*Good boy. But in the meantime, here I am ready to go with nowhere to go. Maybe you could... *

"Puh-leeze!"

We have to do something! What about her?

Enter: A sparkling example of how age is nothing but a number. Dressed in a deep blue skirt suit, medium heels and carrying a big purse, this celestial brunette wonderment in her mid-forties has a bust line not too far behind. The inches across her waist are nearly my age and her hips are swinging. A too-cute chin and obviously in a hurry, I so hate to delay her for her modeling gig.

Jump her!

"Noooooo."

Jump her!

"I said, 'no!'"

Jump her or we do anatomy.

"Excuse me, Miss."

This beauty tarries-not from her high stepping.

"Can I get your attention for a moment or two?"

Or an hour or two?

"Can this wait, young man?"

NO!

"No, not really, ma'am."

"I'm in a major hurry. Give me what you're selling. I'll buy it."

"Selling? Selling? No, ma'am, I just, uh... can we... uh..."

Have sex!

"Have sex?"

"Beg your pardon."

Her high steps are nigh steps. What did I say?

Nothing! Go with the flow and go with her flow!

"Okay. You wanted my attention and you made me late. Let's say we kill three birds with one stone. I'm Kayla."

Three birds? Three birds? Who cares? She is taking her taking off her clothes, though, or at least her coat. She, uh, wants to get it on right here in the street?

No prob.

"Nice to make your acquaintance, Kayla. My name is Dinky."

I remove my shirt, then my shoes. Well, I try to remove my shoes. Stooping to slip off the stubborn slip-ons, a glance at my "partner" lets me notice her in some strange pajamas. White cotton top. Almost like a dress or an oversized cardigan. No buttons on it, though. She has it held closed with a long, black, knotted sash. The top overlaps baggy, capri-length pants made from the same material. Hey, she really has cute calves. Pretty feet, too. Did I get lucky or what?

"Wondering about those three birds," she asks.

"No," I almost smile, "not really. Can I keep my socks on?"

"Sure."

"Ma'am..." what was her name, again? "Kayla! Yeah, Kayla! Why are you bowing?"

"You made me late."

"For what? Dinner at a Thai restaurant?"

No response. Instead she bounces into a, who knows, a Kung Fu fighting stance?

Sex in this new millennium seems to be weirder and weirder.

Anyway, she continues to stand there vulturistic, looking good, poised for hot sex, undressing me with her eyes. Shunning the inhibitions that stopped me from having this encounter with Kismet [and fewer spectators], I strip the pants to give her eyes a break and a view.

"You wanted my attention. That's bird number one."

Birds. Bees. This is great!

"You also made me late for my appointment. You know what that appointment was?"

"Again with the appointment. Tell me! Tell me, what was this appointment?!"

"I'm a Tae Kwon Do instructor. Tonight's my first class. My first class that somebody made me late for."

Silence. Tension. Thick tension.

Three birds? She mentioned three birds. I got her attention. Bird one. Tae Kwon Do instructor. Bird two. What was bird three?

"Get ready for a private lesson. You're bird three!"

"Sex? Who wants sex? Especially here in the street? With all these people driving by...? Hey! Put that foot down! Ughnn!!"

"I'll do the honor of teaching you each strike as it's inflicted. That was a roundhouse kick to the kidney."

"Gee, thanks. Ughnn!"

"Front kick to the solar plex."

"Ughnn! Ughnn! Ughnn!"

"Triple combination punches to the temple, chin and stomach."

Go ahead. Take the punishment. No need to defend yourself.

Listening to Conscience, I mount the intention of bringing an overhand right to her chest. Ulterior motives? Maybe. Anyway, she swerves and... "Ughnn!"

"Front kick to the solar plex."

"You used that already."

"It's my favorite."

"Ughnn!"

"Outside Crescent kick to the forehead. And could you possibly use another expletive denoting a good shot?"

"Sorry, >>koff<<, I can try. Awunfph."

"Spinning back fist to the jaw and thank you."

"You are more than welcome. P-tui!"

"A tooth?"

"Gum."

She withdraws her martial assault, never dropping her poise or positioning.

"Answer a question, please?"

"Let me guess: why am I still standing?"

"You like this attention?"

"Not exactly. My conscience really wants you, which might not happen if I get laid out in the street."

Really?! You pointed her attention at me?!

"I applaud your resilience, but..."

Ughnn!

"I hate to leave a job undone. Front kick to your... conscience."

My knees smack cement. The upper three-fourths double over. She hurt me.

Kayla turns to collect her outerwear, dresses and politely walks over me to resume her original course.

"The next time you stop a woman on the street," she offers, "ask for directions. See you in class?"

>>Koff<<

Is she gone, yet?

"Yeah, but sure as hell not forgotten."

You should have left her alone.

"YOU wanted her!!"

I wanted something other than her feet. Slow feet! Anyway, we have to leave. Protect our future.

"Meaning?"

Get up! Get off the street!

"Do you mind? I would like to collect myself."

Disperse me and the boys turtled up with the prostate and skedaddle elsewhere! Something will happen if you stay doubled over in public!

"In Carlisle? What could happen in Carlisle?"

>>Woowoowooo<<

Hazel.

An hour later, another interrogation. [S]he added to her collection of DinkyBriefs.

Another hour, I think. Learning the trick from Conscience, the shoes are on autopilot. I just want to go. Go somewhere. Who cares where. Shoes? Take me there.

Are you writing a beer commercial?

"Conscience?"

Who else?

"I really can do without you right now."

You realize dude, your other head is a seesaw.

"I hope you have an explanation."

Sure.

"Hold it a sec. Why do I feel you should be wrapping one arm around my shoulder, prodding me forward, while using the other, free-waving arm, to help paint the images?"

I could wrap what I do have around your shoulder.

"Forget I asked."

I will.

"This seesaw thing?"

It is your mind. Your mind with a lone, little kid on one side of it. Call this kid, 'Sanity.'

"I hope this kid has a nickname."

Are you following me?

"I guess."

Then shut up. Now, this kid on your mental balance is so small, he can play on it by himself, staying on just the one side.

My bruised forehead drops, flinting the hint of a spark of a response.

I said shut up! As the kid is playing with himself, hmmmmm, a big, dumpy, big, lumpy, big, huge, dumpy, hyperthyroid, pre-adolescent bully, i.e., your life experiences, plunks his chunk on the opposite seesaw side, thus sending Sanity auditioning for NASA. Understand?

"No."

You will if you want to survive.

Food for thought. Probably something Mom cooked.

My shoes, still on autopilot, have carried me to another time zone. Another hour, possibly? Who cares? Why bother? What is my purpose? Read my lips, no new taxes?

Gosh, I hate my life. I hate the bully on the seesaw.

"Mmmph! What the..."

A door? My shoes directed me to a door? A nice door? A very nice door? Jabbing repeatedly at this entrance with fingers spread wide, the complete composition stays foreign to my touch. The rebounding sound waves offer little help for recognition, either. I can figure out where I am later. Right now, I have to know what this door is made of.

Hold it.

>>Smik<<>>t-chit<<>>chank<<

A SecuriTech chain/deadbolt superlock system set?

The doorknob turns. Soon, the owner of the mysterious door can answer questions about this marvel. It creaks open. Opener... and opener... and...

"Russell? Is this your door?"

"Goes with the house."

"Yeah. I see. What material is this made from?"

"Can we do this tomorrow, Dink?"

"Why? Oooh, were you in bed?"

"What gave it away? The pajamas?"

No! Not more pajamas!

"Why're you knocking at this hour?"

"What hour?"

"3:15 in the morning."

"Time goes by fast when having crises, man."

Apparently, humor does not please my friend at 3:15 in the morning. He retroactively assumes a staunch, deep and transcendental disposition.

"Dink," he softly terrorizes.

"Yyyyyyyes?" softerly sobbing.

"Go. Home."

"Why do you think I am out at this hour? Th-The people there..."

"Are your family."

"Please," sobbing softestly, "give me a better reason."

"Pepper."

Literally probing jaggedly for pepper's significance...

"Pepper has no nutritional value. Didn't know that, did you?"

Still probing. A feverish glance picks up a calm, cognizant glow through his face.

"What're you thinking now, my friend?"

Only my stare has more void.

"Trust me. Go home."

I hate it when he does that: derailing me and then loading a newer, cleaner transporter on the tracks. If he could replace the conductor...

"The man in the funny hat is more than capable, Dink."

"Akkk. I think... uh... uh... I think I better... leave. Yeah. Go home. Like you said. Go home. My family... they live next door, you know?"

"Dink, shut up and go home."

"Yeah... I think I can..."

>>Slam<<

"Go home."

>>Knock<< >>Knock<< >>Knock<<

"Russell! Open up, man!"

>>Knock<< >>Knock<< >>Knock<< >>Knock<< >>Knock<< >>Knock<<

"Rus-sellllllllllllllllllllllllllllllllllllllllllllllllll!"

The massive door, barely a day old, opens. Standing behind it? A young man so mad, his eyebrows hang low enough to pose as a beard.

"I… said… go..."

He stops cold. His brows recoil.

"Why don't you come in," he sings. "Let's see if you learned anything."

"Thankyou, thankyou, huh?"

"This way."

He revolves and walks into the house, talking behind him.

"Care to... go somewhere, Dink?"

The house's complete lack of light keeps me mere steps away from the front door.

"Yeah. Can I stay here? How long will it take you to get ready?"

"Yes and gimme half."

The darkness swallows him.

"30 minutes?! Why so long?"

No response. Just dark.

"Russell? Russell?"

Dark.

"Russell, can I turn on the..."

>>click<<

"Grrrrr!"

"Hi, Apocalypse," resobbing softestly.

Collecting myself, I open my mouth to scream and, instead, hear a sigh. What good would a scream do anyway?

Apocalypse jumps at me. Definitely having no time for a countdown, >>qra-CHOOOOM<<. Door number eight never makes it out of neonatal. Thankfully, I called that temporary body fluid employment agency for some adrenaline. Good stuff, too.

Making it across the yards to my own front door... no dog, no pain. Whoa.

And since it is 3:20 in the a.m., maybe sleeping at this reasonable hour seems... reasonable.

I reach my front door. I reach for the door. I open the door. No tingly teeth. Oh yeah, this is my moment. Good adrenaline-for-hire, a decent bedtime and Pops drowses? What a night! Good night!

Not so fast, Main. Dinky Control here. That temporary Adrenaline collapsed from exhaustion. Do you copy?

Oh, please. Oh, please, no. Hold on. Please, hold on. Just a few more steps. Come on, Dinky. One... more... damn.

"Aaaaaaaaarrrrrg-oompf!!!!"

>>Bamp<< >>BampBamp<< >>Bamp<<

How many...

>>Bamp<<

steps are there?

>>BampBampBampBamp<< >>Bamp<< >>Bamp<< >>Bamp<< >>BampBamp<< >>BAMMM<<

Fifteen.

Wondering if this counts as throwing myself down the stairs, the expected comes.

"Shut up, boy! Folks're tryin' ta sleep!"

Yeah. Like me. Right here. In the foyer. Good night and let the good snooze be yours.

THIS CHAPTER

Author's note: What's up? I'm presently "available," because our erstwhile patriarch has the attentiveness of cold cod. Slept the whole night where he landed. Not a pretty sight either. All bent up. Joints folded in directions they weren't meant to.

Ouch.

He'll have kinks. Nasty, awful kinks. When he jettisons off the doze dock, pain's gonna slap him like a sleazebag lawyer in a Hollywood paternity suit.

The calendar made its final farewells to yesterday. Wednesday. A date never to pass this way again. The day, though, was quite typical for The Dink. Tomorrows are for the fortunate and today is the last day for the rest of his life. The weather? Overcast. Mr. Richard Deankey? Overcaster.

He'll be real pissed I'm here. So what. I presently have the power to manipulate people and situations to my liking. The Other Guy, specifically. Dinky, himself, is nothing more than my puppet for profit. Those human rights activists complained that I shouldn't use this sap, no matter how stupid. Right? Right?

Puh-leeze, as he would say. You use people and love it! You'd love it more if you got paid for it!

Alas, let's curtail this instant epistemology [get a dictionary] and concentrate on Dinky. Gotta get up, he does, he does. Perhaps, manipulating his mother, having her approach him and...

"Richard? I made breakfast."

It didn't work! It didn't work? Sure shocks my she-bees. Okay, send the woman kitchen-ward. I'll use her again shortly.

Man, it almost hurts watching him crinkled up like that, but not as much as it will him. Gotta wake him, though. What if...

"Hey dude, your clothes are wrinkled."

"Nnnngh."

Bingo. And here comes the pain.

"Aaaaaaaaaaaaaaaaaaaaaaaaaaaaaaaaaaaaa..."

>>snit<< >>tst<< >>snap<< >>stst<< >>crackle<< >>POP<<

"Quit bugging me, boy!"

I love this job.

What the...? The foyer? How did I...

"NO! My clothes! I slept in them! Aw man, wrinkles! If anybody sees me like this..."

Instant-presto-change-o.

"Whew."

Descending the stairway, I glance around, making certain no one saw me crinkley-like. The small droplets on my foreheadial region – representing a non-thorough toweling after showering – remind me to show you the shower Swydni installed. By the way, I look good again, proving nobody knows green... like Dinkers.

A short sleeve button-down, printed shirt, tailored shorts and name brand walking shoes. No socks, but plenty of flesh-colored foot powder.

I limp past the collection bucket, trying to remember if the rent paid itself. Did I pay rent today? I paid yesterday, but today is a new today, as opposed to an old today, which I would have paid on when it was new, therefore, since today is new, paying now before it gets old will keep me in line before the old today turns new.

Pay the rent.

The wallet grips my attention. It gets gripped, searching for that legal folding tender that stops Ma and Pa from gripping my throat. Putting Mom's gift on one hip – slightly crumpled by last night's stairway tumble – and reaching deep in the other, fabricked hip, a noise grips my notice.

>>Splish<<

Splish? What the...? Water? A bunch of it, too. I better get a mop before...

"Oonf."

An uncharted edifice in the foyer blocks my mission. Looking up reveals and unveils an identity and anxieties.

"Pops?"

"Where'syourmother,boy?"

The man... drips. Figuratively worse than me. This gravitating, heavy humidity also describes my situation and my feelings, because Mommy's fish are now sacrificial lambs, shoved in his face to buy escape seconds.

>>Rrrrrr-unch!!!<<

He bit them.

"Where'syourmother,boy?"

"Umm," groping hard for an answer. No luck.

"Boy?"

Uh oh. Divert his drive.

"Pops!!! What happened?!!! Why are you wet?!!!"

"New attachment on the toilet."

"Moooooooooooooooooooooooooooooooom!!!"

The object of our afflictions rounds the corner into the foyer, garbed in her combat kitchen apron, gloves a friend "borrowed" from a nuclear plant and goggles. She is armed with a smoldering, blackened, heavy metal spatula.

"What's all the commotion, Richard?"

The situation hits her like a ton of brisket.

"Oscar. Honey. You're wet."

"Uh huh," he drools.

"Later, honey. After breakfast."

"Take her, Pops!!! Take her!!!"

"Oscar, please. Oscar? Oscar?!"

He stalks her. Her weak pleas for carnal leniency mean nothing. Like a caveman deprived of raw meat for far too long, he stalks his prize.

"Oscar!"

>>Shnikt<<

Using the smoking utensil, Mom sent a wicked forehand to Pops' left cheek. Although, he currently sports a perfect, black square temp tat with a lovely floral design in the middle, the assault had no effect.

"Oscar!"

>>Shnikt<<>>Shnikt<<

Whoa! An awesome backhand/forehand combination to the temples. These new tats also had no effect as he scoops her up and heads for the tub.

"Oscar!"

>>Shnikt<<

"Oscar!"

>>Shnikt<<>>Shnikt<<

"Oscar!"

>>Shnikt<<

"Noooooo!"

>>Slam<<

The bedroom door.

>>Slam<<

The bathroom door. And...

>>SPLASH<<

"Oscar!"

What? No shnikt?

"Oscar! Yes, Oscar! Oooh, yes, Oscar!"

Puh. Leeze. Those people rarely represent the contemporary at all. Their NC17-rated, 1950s sitcom almost churns my stomach enough to keep me from the kitchen.

Almost.

"Smavic? Time."

"Ten-thirty-one a.m. Thursday."

Hmmm. Not exactly breakfast, but too soon for lunch. Sort of like the breakfast hamburger/lunch hamburger change-over time at Mackey's.

No prob. I can brunch it.

Heading for food, Mom should be tied up long enough for me to spit fry a pig, because Pops be not a minuteman.

Going through the living room/museum, I recall him telling me how bubbles put him in a frenzy, which makes him "generate" more bubbles, which frenzies him more, etceteras, etceteras, etceteras. Why he told me such a thing probably classifies somewhere near male-bonding. And hey, when a bigger man starts bonding thusly, you shut up, praying his attention stays on his memories.

Globuly speaking, about nine or ten years ago Mom was washing the car where she made the mistake of throwing a bucket of sudsy water on it. Pops jumped her right there on the trunk. Being a football Sunday, of course the police were called. The only body-bumping relationships any other neighborhood man wanted even know about was to be those on their television.

The officers were destined to fail, though, subdued by the crowd of horny wives who gathered in the front yard cheering Pops on.

Anyway, the creeks and snaps you would hear if this were a movie [some nine years later, i.e., right now] is not me walking on the hardwood floors. Primarily, because we have none. No, see, I slept in the foyer, remember?

And who woke me up???

In the kitchen, Mom's gourmet interpretation of L.A. atmosphere simulates the outside gloom. Or does the outside imitate the in? Either way, I relish the time granted to cook a feast without having to pay for it. Prepare it and sneak out, even with the foreseeable trouble soon to be mentioned:

Swydni!

She sits opposite the breakfast bar, staring over a whatchamacallit. It could be another one of her inventions, were it plugged in. A small... stack? Hard to tell.

She acknowledges my entrance.

"Hrrmmmph."

Always glad to see me, she is.

"What do you have there, Sis?"

"Why?"

"Answer the question," annoying me to no end.

"Something... I made for home ec."

"Mom charge you for using her kitchen?"

"You're the only one she does that way."

True.

Encompassing the bar, I position myself behind her and lean over her shoulder. Getting closer hardly makes the stuff in front of her any more recognizable. Not at all, really.

"Hungry, Brother?"

Should I take note of her slight, sudden sarcasm? Maybe next time.

"What is that?"

"Uh, pancakes."

"Green pancakes, Swydni? You took home ec. pass/fail, right?"

"It's the mint syrup," she says, maintaining her focus on the jade mound.

"What mint syrup?"

"The mint syrup... these pancakes soaked up."

Alright. She has something other than flapjacks cooking here. What is she up to? Does the stomach care?

"Oookaaay, Sis. Why are you giving me green pancakes? Why even offer me your food before I ritually take it, thereby continuing the traditional big brother/little sister status."

"Well, Dumpy..."

"Dinky, dammit."

"Uh huh, yeah. Anyway, I'm done. Y'know? Done eating."

"You just made this."

2 plus 2?

"Can't a girl change her mind? Here. Take it."

Swydni slides the it on the bar over a bit. I pull out the chair and sit down in front of... it. Do I eat it? Do I kill her? Decisions. Decisions. Looking back and forth from her to it, logic steps in and speaks.

"Fork?"

"Be a man, Dinkoid. Use your hands."

"I will," raspberrying her. "So, there."

Why did Mom and Pops stop me from selling her when she was a baby? Oh, well.

Reluctantly biting the big bite, the taste of mint julep is... is... Hello? Minty flavor? Where are you? Hmmm, I do encounter crunches. Either from the crêpe suzettes or this creep's zootonomy?

Chewing the big chew, I assume the pancakes hide the mint syrup like a piece of gum. Chew. Nothing. Chew. Nothing. Chew.

"Richard!"

Damn.

Hearing that word in this room instinctively sends the hand wallet-ward. Panning toward the source of the verbal force displays an interesting sight: Mom swaggering into the room like a bad actor playing drunk. Her body wearing more water than clothes. She must have been...

No. I will not complete that thought.

"Richard? Why're you eating my cookie dough?"

"What?!" I cry, spitting out new thoughts and words and whatever else is in my mouth.

"Why're you eating my Christmas cookie dough, Richard?" she sloshes.

"Mom, Christmas is two seasons away!"

"By then, Richard, it'll turn red."

"Mom," feeling serious sweat, "Swydni made these! She called them pancakes!"

The 2 plus 2 is coming. I know it.

"Richard," sighing out of pity, which happens a lot to me, "why would anybody eat pancakes on a napkin?"

4! Scream! Nope! No good!

Unfortunately, the metamorphisizing cookie clog expands, lodging my mouth airtight. Breathing nasally prescribes the next logical respiratory step, but the actuality of consuming one of Mom's counterfeit food-matters detours all synapses.

Remarkable as it is to say, breathing represents the least of my concerns. Again, consuming one of Mom's fake foods depicts the biggie. That means, what takes place in the four-minute absence of oxygen will now happen a whole lot sooner:

———————— **BLACKOUT** ————————

We reserve the right to use this page for dreaming.

Author's note: What's up with this guy? This... this Other Guy? It's bad enough he started the chapter comatose. Now, he's been tricked into eating something his Mom made? I tell you, he may have book sense, but he ain't got a lick of common.

Yeah, his inner-head's kind of squishy, but you can still learn a lot about the man by being in there. Probably more than he admits about himself. Probably more than he understands about himself.

When you're dreaming, most times you don't know that you're actually dreaming even when it's the fantastic dream. A crème de la dream. A dream's dream's dream.

In [t]his dream, everything's going great. Like many dreams, you brave the last most intensely imagined thought before hitting the hay. Despite the fact he seldom mentions it, what Dinky most intensely thinks about most is more than virginity absenteeism.

He's a romantic. Hard to guess? True. I know. I know this guy. He wants the perfect situation to lose his virginity, not making it seem like he's just losing his virginity. Instead, voyaging on lifehood's next degree of education or educational degree.

Whatever.

Your greatest desire may seek a different school. Dinky, more often than he wants, finds himself enrolled at "Intensely Wanting To Have Sex University." More aptly named, "I Wanna Screw U."

He's dreaming. He's dreaming about himself as the ideal man in a very sweet, touching encounter with a particular person of the female species. He desires her. He wants nothing more than to see her have a great deal of pleasure. He wants to give her that pleasure, while, as a side note, get his kicks, too.

His kicks really aren't important. Not to him. Not at the present. He wants them inevitably, realizing it would culminate into that ridiculous cherry topping on the perfect sundae. The totality of it all pretty much cultivates the love/lust thing for him.

Dinky's philosophy on consummating consummatable relationships has simplicity: Making love is like two snackaholics in a grocery store: you're not finished until you both get your cookies.

He currently dreams about insuring his lover enjoys a chocolate chunk cookie the size of Montana. He'll settle for a petit four. It matters very little to him. To make the dessert reality, so to speak, he'll do whatever it takes.

All this food talk is making me hungry.

Returning to the original premise, you don't know you're dreaming, rhapsodizing greatly, until somebody wakes you up, waking you at the exact moment absolutely necessary – mandatory – for the complete fantasy.

Kismet will soon nibble on her cookie, a county at a time. In fact, Dinky's about to get his, too, when... it's time to wake up.

He'll also hate where his mother took him.

"Mistuh? >>snif<< Mistuh? Mistuh?"

Hold it. No. No. No! NO! Please! Let me keep the dream a little longer! Please!

Okay. Calm down, Dinky man. Calm down. I can bring it back. Eyes closed. Breathe. Yes. Bring it back. Yeah. Almost. Almost. Alllllllmossst.

"Mistuh?"

Mistuh? Huh? Damn! Lost it! Man, that was a good... dream? Oh man, I was dreaming? When did I go to bed?

>>Sigh<<

What happened to me this time?

Before liberating the observation glands, the other senses have downloaded their info regarding my surroundings, especially the ears.

The sounds of sniffles. Way too many kids annoying the significant adult in their lives. Building blocks being forced together. The smells of copycat perfumes, smelling nothing like what they copycat. The smell of diaper rash and diapers filled. The smell of mentholated vapor rub. The feel of waiting room chairs.

"Mistuh?"

And that dad-blasted, "Mistuh."

Disengage eyes.

"Mom, no! Not here!! Pediatrics?!!! Mom!!!!"

I should have finished those thoughts in my head.

"Hi. Please, do not mind me. Take care of your kids. The ones you all just snatched. I will sit here turning red, were I not over-charged, pigmentationally speaking."

They return to their mundane. Good. I can return to mine. Hmmm. More fathers here than usual.

Mom took me to pediatrics, keeping the mouth closed while my temperature rises.

What time is it?

"Smavic...?"

Oops. Forgot.

"Go on back to your own worlds, people."

Silently searching for the time of day, the customary hospital big clock points the big hand at twelve, the little one at two.

Two o'clock? What was I doing? Why am I even here? Two o'clock. What was I doing? I was talking... no. Talking to... no. Hold it. Start at the beginning: Woke up. Wrinkled clothes.

"Wrinkled clothes?!!!"

Did the scream or the body-languaged punctuation do it?

"Normally, people pay big money for my brand of entertainment. I can give you all the group rate."

Good. Now, back to the recant: Wrinkled clothes. Pops. Splish. Him. Mom. Hot tub. Kitchen. Swydni. Green pancakes. Cookie dough.

"No!!!"

Damn.

"Okay. Looking this way again will cost you five bucks apiece."

Nosy so-and-so's. By the way, where is Mom?

"Mistuh?"

Oh, puh-leeze. Just what I need, a snotty brat tugging my shorts.

"Mistuh?"

"Yeah, little one? What do you want?"

"Is yur kid inna, >>snif<<, in the doktur's room? Screaming his head off?"

"No. That munchkin screams a whole octave lower than I do."

The way this kid looks at me, my comment definitely slid off his back rather than sailed over his head.

"Where is your kid, mistuh?"

Who is this kid? About five years old, presumably, and wearing tennis shoes I would never buy a child. Name brand. Ninety-five bucks, if a penny. He does have the coolest, purple, short-pant bib overalls. One side not latched. A back-in-the day style, indeed.

Is he...? Yukk. Wiping his nose with his arm, smearing it on his shirt? His shirt that changes colors at the touch? Either he has a touch-sensitive shirt or he can see the doctor before me. Way before me.

"Mistuh?"

I should tell him my name, because I hate the way he says...

"Mistuh?"

"Dinky!"

"Mistuh Dinky?"

"No, kid. Call me Dinky?"

"Dinky? Where's your kid?"

"I... ummm... not here with me."

"Oh. Are you sick?"

"Depends on who you ask."

"Huh," he snots.

"Forget it. Hey! Did I have something in my mouth when I came here?"

"Uh huh. A blue, shiny thing."

Blue? Shiny? Do not ask. Do. Not. Ask.

"What happened to it?"

Damn. I asked.

"A couple people chipped some of it outta yur mouth. They said you swallowed the ress."

Ugh.

"Okay then, kid? Where is the stuff they chipped out?"

"My liddle brother's playin' wif it. >>snif<< Over there."

Pointing in the direction of the previously mentioned building block banging, my glossy companion attentions me toward a smaller version of himself. A smaller, less glossy version, pulverizing inaccurately-believed, sturdy Legos. Mom's cookie dough obviously makes a great hammer. The color is different, but it is definitely her dough.

"Mistuh?"

"Call me Dinky."

"Dinky? Where's your kid?"

"Are we back to this? My... uh... boy's grandma is bringing him. Yeah. They wanted to meet me here."

"What's his name?" he innocently asks.

Pause.

For some reason, fuel for the lies evaporates. A name. Any name. Say a name. Instead, I snicker reflectantly. Probably body-languaged it, too. But the kid's innocent question raises a paternal urge.

Hopefully, someday.

"Why are you here, little one? Got a cold?"

"No. Mommy works in the building. Everybody knows me an' my brother. When Mommy brings us wif her, we pick the floor we wanna be on and they babysit us."

"What about your father?"

"Don't got none."

Hopefully, someday.

"Mommy tells me not to talk to strangers," now negligibly avid. "She's comin' up here."

"Then how do you make friends with the kids having doctor's appointments?"

"I think she means adult strangers."

"Oh. And you can tell she is coming?"

"Experience."

What a gem his mother has.

"For yur entertainment, Dinky, the lobby offers a vawiety of magazines."

"You do come here often."

"Uh huh. I gotta go. Nice talkin' to ya Mistuh Dinky."

"Hey. You never told me your name."

"You didna ask," he cutely sniffs.

"What is your name, little one?"

"July."

"Where you born then?"

"No, Auguss. Gotta go, Mistuh Dinky. Bye."

He motions for his brother and out the door they go, both apparently reaching for the hands of the lady who brought them.

Hopefully, July. Hopefully, someday in the near future.

Big hand on six. Little hand between the three and four. Five hours lost, most of it in a doctor's office. A doctor's office where I sit by myself, taking my little new friend's advice.

"For my amusement..." he said. I end up reading every magazine ever put in a pediatrician's waiting room, including the one with the purple dinosaur, and an assortment of coloring books, which, yes, I colored.

After a few minutes – twenty, to be exact – the building blocks amused me. The surviving ones July's brother failed to granulate.

Mom's cookie dough stayed intact. Seems bigger, too.

Unexplainable to me, reading re grabs my fundamental wants. Sneaking into OB/GYN, the magazine nearest the entrance disappears.

Yeah, blame me. Go ahead.

Resting comfortably in the chair which understands my butt print best, I unfold the literature that magically showed up in this waiting room. Hmmm, *Illustrating Sports*? Not exactly the expected material in an office that predominantly caters to women, assuming it came from there, of course.

I flip through it. Flip. Flip. Huh? The advertisement for their swimsuit issue – more than a quite a few months away – did hook me. The article on pre-pre-professional basketball reeled me in:

Before The NBA
In the concrete jungle, beneath the steel high-rises, the sun boroughs a path to the basketball courts in graffitied neighborhoods. There, it finds a smaller orb waiting for him. Daybreak initiates fast breaks as those aspiring to play in Madison Square Garden bleak the reality on Madison and Fifth Avenue. But smog black tops must release their monopoly of big dreams and bigger checks to the snow courts of Indiana, the copper wire spools living a second life as a backboard in Texas and the no bounce sand lots of California. Basketball's greatest hail from these unrefined resources. Future generations will repeat the trek.

Read. Flip. Read. Flip. Hmmm!

This story makes me think. Translatingly speaking, time for another story: A basketball game, pretty much like the ones in the article. Lorenzo fouled Eugene or vice versa. Anyway, a heated argument ensued and Lorenzo left the court. Eugene figured he went after his gun and went home for his.

Later the same day, when the incident seemed forgotten, we, or more precisely, they crossed paths at a private party on the outer reaches of town. Lorenzo had one of his normal vivacious "escorts" on his arm. Entering the party, he literally bumped into Eugene. Lorenzo, weaponless, pushed his date aside and stared down the barrel of Eugene's Glock. The woman's dress split open across the breasts. Her assets caught Eugene's attention. Lorenzo snatched his gun and shot at him.

Empty.

Pissed, Lorenzo went to hit his adversary across the temple with the gun when it went off. The bullet parted Eugene's hair real deep. Since the party was very private, all the witnesses who did not drink a fifth took the Fifth and the incident was officially reported as self-inflicted.

"Are you alright, sir?"

Uh oh. Despite being completely absorbed in my thoughts, I realize this question comes from somebody in the real world and is rhetorical.

Hold it. Something too nice smells too familiar.

"Sir?"

Better spry up and face reality. Slowly, Dinky, slowly. Bring the real world into focus and...

Impressive.

Standing before me, a woman old enough to be my mother, yet attractive enough not to be. She possesses something maternal about her. Perhaps the polyester hospital uniform that always looks a tad maternal... or funereal. In my case, the two co-mingle.

This lady, though, could have easily been a high school prom queen. Either that or a former blimp. Perhaps a weight-loss program spokesperson, like the kind on television who stands next to a life-size picture of their ex-Goodyear self, eating a stove.

5'3". Big, brown eyes. Short, brown hair. Caucasian with light brown skin. About 115 brown pounds.

"I'm sorry you've waited this long for the doctor," she captivates.

"I understand."

"Really?"

"Uh uh. Why the wait?"

"Thursday's are usually his worst day. To make matter worse, he had a couple emergency operations between golf rounds."

"Pretty serious, huh?"

"Slightly."

Quite adorable, the woman before me.

"It backlogs his schedule. And since you came in without an appointment... you're last. Usually, being last doesn't mean being this late. Again, I apologize."

"No problem. Really."

"Forgive my rudeness," she humbles, extending a greeting hand. "I'm Mae."

"Dinky," shaking. "No, Richard," still shaking. "No, Dopey," shaking still. "No..."

"You can keep my hand, but settle on one name."

"Pick one," unshaking, "or make one up."

She laughs. Is it possible for me to admire a woman without lusting for her?

"I better get back to my station. I'll see what I can do."

"Thanks, Mae."

I wait.

Big hand on six. Little hand splitting the four and five. Here comes Mae.

"The doctor will see you now."

About %&#@@* time.

My escort shows me into a room. Before closing the door behind her, she instructs me to remove my shirt and that the doc will be in shortly.

I do. Then sit on the paper-covered bed. Then survey the room. Ah, more magazines.

Different clock. Big hand on three. Little hand off the six. Where is the doctor?

New magazine. Big hand on the nine. Little hand on the... on the... on the zzzzz... zz zzzz zzzzzz zzzzzzzzzzzzzzzzzzzzzzzzzzzzzzzzzzzzzzzzzzzzzz.

"Mr. Deankey?"

"No, not that kid again."

"Wake up, Mr. Deankey, or I'll have to charge you for spending the night."

Spending the night?

"Wake up, man."

Erecting like the Frankenstein monster first did, I slowly aim my cognate attention at the man dressed bad. His clipboard clashes, he dresses so bad.

"It's alive!"

"Not funny, Doc. Is it really morning?"

"Afraid so."

"Why am I still here? Where the hell have you been?"
"Emergency overnight golf tournament."

Golf. That explains his clothes. What it could never explain is why these men – who use a heavy-ended, graphite stick to inevitably slice or hook a small, over-dimpled ball standing on a wood peg in a perfectly tended to, large, green plot – dress horrendously.

Honestly, in the same fashion as the goose that laid the golden eggs – no pun intended – when golf shipped its way to America, somebody already in the states stumbled across an intergalactic alien who hurled chunks, which this somebody draped over clothes hangers, stood on Plymouth Rock and waited for some Scottish suckers.

"How are you feeling, Mr. Deankey?"

After giving my opinionated testimony...

"Tired."

"I'll include the stay on your bill, after all. These notes here," going through his clipboard, "say you swallowed a basketball."

"No, my mother's Christmas cookie dough."

"Mr. Deankey," he condescends, "Christmas is two seasons away."

"I know that!!!"

"Calm down. Have you, ummm, eaten anymore basketballs in the last twelve hours?"

"No! I have been here since eleven yesterday morning!"

"Are you hungry?"

"Yeah," loudly protesting.

"Then I suggest you patronize a fast food restaurant. You're free to go."

"What?!!"

"You're free to go."

"What?" preparing for an emotional performance. "I sat here overnight. You walk in dressed like hell, wearing sandalistic golf shoes and without running one test, tell me I can go?"

"Care to stay another day?"

Silence.

"Then git outta here!"

Taking the doctor's "advice," I don my shirt and cower from his office, almost graciously accepting the bill he hands me.

I head downstairs, pay the cashier and leave through the main lobby, grumbling the whole time about what I went through.

Did I pass Mae?

Approaching the final exit, a woman who looks behind in her schedule comes at me. Trying to remember that Tae Kwon Do instructor, I think: "Let her pass. Let her..."

"Mae?"

"Dinky? You had another appointment?"

"I never left the first one."

"I'm sorry. Didn't I leave you with the doctor?"

"He had a late emergency."

"I'm sorry. Listen, I really have to go. See you around?"

"I pray for it."

And really, I do. But anyway, what was I doing...? Doors? Yeah.

Opening the exit, city sounds overwhelm. No, not city sounds. Car crashes. In the distance, I hear a lot of angry motorists. Sounds that make a lot of sense if one particular person presently operates a motor vehicle.

Jussst as I step to the curb, a familiar car with unfamiliar dents and scratches screeches to a halt in front of me. And out pops... you guessed it. Full of glee and drenched.

"Hi, Richard. Am I late?"

A CHAPTER

"Am I late, Richard?"

Dumbfounded. One way or another, this woman leaves me dumbfounded.

"Are you ready, Richard?"

Somebody smite me. Blow away the remaining ashes. Remove the tiniest micro-essence, period.

"Mom," trying to extract the fly why's with a sugar voice rather than with my real vinegar verve, "you understand this is... THE DAY AFTER!!!!!!"

So the verve came forth.

"It is, Richard?"

Oh, clouds? My smite, please.

"Oh, Richard. Your father... ohhhhhhhhhh."

"I was going to ask you about the suds," which she absolutely glows through.

By the way, this entire "exchange" takes place with we participants leaning on top of the family wreckage. Apparelly speaking, I could use her to squeegee this beast clean. Anyway, an angry mob of unscheduled pedestrians sprint toward us from the direction she came from.

"There she is! Kill her!"

Yep. Unscheduled pedestrians. Carrying flaming mufflers.

"Made any friends driving lately, Mom?"

"Get in the car, Richard."

Clinched teeth give her the conversational upper hand.

In the car. Possibly upset, she is the Ivory woman. 44/100ths pure and foaming. Actually, Mom usually stays mad or upset about a half minute, tops. Then her fury dissipates completely, unless she has something she can throw. Things like plates, lawn darts, furniture, me, Pops, etc.

So, she has obviously water polo-ed and she looks worse for washing. In fact, the only time she looked worse was when Russell came over and we stumbled upon Jell-o boxes everywhere. Seriously. Everywhere.

Everywhere!

Whatever dark emotions she carried before we sped off, she left back on the curb. Me? Uh uh. She left me in pediatrics overnight, remember?

A few blocks and a couple side-swipes later, she breaks the silence.

"Richard...?"

Pissed-off progeny stare glues the silence back together.

Moments later, after locking bumpers with a fire engine...

"I liked your present, Richard."

Where are we going?

"Richard, I liked your present."

"Huh?"

"Thanks, Richard."

"For what?"

"The gift, Richard. The aquarium."

"Am I mad at you?"

"How, Richard? You bought me a birthday present."

Am I missing something?

"Richard? Can I let you in on a secret?"

"Only if you have to."

"You might've noticed, for all practical purposes, Richard..."

"Yeah, Mom?"

"For all practical purposes, Richard..."

"You said that already."

"What I'm trying to say, Richard, is... I can't cook!"

"And?"

"That's it, Richard. I can't cook. Over the years, I've hid it pretty well. That is, if you don't include the various home renovations and testing the upper limits of our health insurance."

Will she get to the point today?

"What I'm saying, Richard, is... I'm trying. My cooking lacks credibility..."

And edibility.

"But I try, Richard. Hopefully, I'll get it right someday. I do know that if I don't try, I'll never get it right."

"So in the meantime, the kitchen keeps the chemical hazards signs?"

"Yes, Richard."

>>Sigh<<

"This isn't about my cooking, Richard. It's about giving up."

"Mom, assuming I had a clue to what you mean, what do you mean?"

"I'm your mother, right, Richard?"

Too easy.

"Mothers have an information network much more intense than any country's government. We also know our children better than they give us credit for. If I stop cooking, Richard, if I give up, it'll be worse than never trying."

Network? Children? Cooking? With her, they almost tie together.

"Mom? What are you talking about?"

"Richard, it's better to have loved and lost than to never have loved at all."

Lights on. Nobody home.

"If you've loved and lost, you get to keep the memories. Memories that not only sustain, but memories that help filter through the malarkey. Help you find what you want, Richard. What you really want."

"What are you talking about?"

"Don't give up, Richard."

"Cooking or loving?"

She smiles. Her body gives a little laughing bounce. She turns to me, tilting her head down a touch. Just a touch. She believes I understand.

Do I?

Yeah. I love this woman...

"Whoa!"

>>Vroommm<< >>Rrrrrsch<<

But not her driving.

"Keep your eyes on the road, Mom!"

"Don't give up, Richard."

"Stay in your lane!"

"Richard. Don't give up."

"Concentrate on driving!"

"Okay, Richard."

"Cool."

Smiles.

"Mom? Could you drop me off at Russell's? In one piece?"

"Aren't you hungry, Richard? Let me cook you breakfast."

"You charging me for it?"

She leers at me. Okay, stupid Q.

"Just drop me off."

Scene change: Russell's bedroom. Mrs. Russell left before I arrived. The automatic visitor system lets me in. Sequelly speaking, another item for future discussions.

In Russell's room, he toils at his computer workstation again, probably finishing up the designs for another patent, netting more money, more money, more money. When I entered his chamber, he glanced at me, possibly preparing for our traditional "greetings." But the thought of him whipping out a Vasectomy Swiss Army Knife curtailed my greeting desire.

Hey! Could I have matured recently, learning and growing away from these juvenile antics? Possibly, although everyone in my world would conceivably answer...

Puh-leeze!

Something bothers me, though. Things have added up lately. Not any two plus two's, but something.

I have a problem. Oh, you figured it out, huh? Well actually, I have many problems which could be tied to one thing. If I picked up a consolidating loan to rectify the big one, then Russell's problem-solving financial agency could satisfy the many smaller problems; therefore, my big problem can get my complete attention while he tackles my smaller ones, which I am actually solving through him, because I am paying him to help me solve my smaller problems, which he helps to group into one big problem, so to speak.

"Russell?" steady at his computer. "Russell?"

"Problem, Dink?"

"Yeah... hey! Stop doing that!"

"Okay. I won't."

He returns his attention back to his computer. He never even turned his body to me. And now, he ignores me totally.

"Russell? Russell? Alright, you win. Tell me my problem, Russell. Russell?!"

"How much time do you have?"

"Russell!"

Pause.

He pushes himself away from his workstation like he had too much to eat. Swivels the chair. Faces me. Stands up. Raises hand. Opens mouth. Sits back down.

Pause.

"My friend, what you see of life, you take too serious."

Huh?

"What I see...?"

"You take too serious."

"No, Russell. What do you mean, 'what I see?'"

"How much time do you have?"

"Russell, man! Kill that line!"

"You need a victory, my friend. One victory... at least to finish off that big problem."

"Big problem?"

"Yeah, Dink. Of course, you'll require a better mind frame."

"Meaning?"

"You'll see when you get home."

"Are you kicking me out."

"In two words?"

"Yeah."

"Bye, Dink."

"What about my problem? My biggest problem? My biggest problem that I can get a loan approved for?"

"One victory. You only need one victory."

"Are you going to tell me?"

"We'll settle it tonight."

"Tonight?" wavering scared. "What about tonight?"

"We're going out."

"Awww, no. No, no, no, no, no!"

"You asked me what your problem was."

"And we have to go out? To that... that place, probably."

"You have a problem with that... that place?"

Another pause.

I hate his cool persona.

I stand, immediately pacing. Is there a problem? Is there a problem?

"Yeah! I have a problem with that place!"

"One victory."

"One victory? W-w-w-what are my problems?!!"

"Go home, Dink. Accept what came in and gear up."

"Gear up?"

"One victory."

"Russell...?"

"Bye, Dink."

Stares.

Physically, I can stare down at him. It is the only way I can stare down at him. And he knows it, too.

"Bye, Dink. Gear up."

On that note, he returns to his workstation and strikes a button. The robotic floor lamps appear, physically suggesting that they will escort me from the premises. Apparently, the automatic visitor system has an exiting program, too.

On the way out, I muse on "one victory" and "gearing up."

"Grrr."

"Huh? Oh. Hi Apocalypse. Tell these things to stop pushing me!"

"Hrrrrrff?"

"Stay there. In fact, all of you stay where you are. I can see myself out."

At the end of the steps, I open the door and walk out. Hmmm. I open the door and walk out. Did I miss something? What just happened?!

Later. At home. In the foyer. Crossing into domestic tribulations. Here comes number one:

Swydni. Carrying something like a shirt box. Wrapped.

"This came in for you."

"What is it?"

"You really wanna know?"

"Yeah, Swydni. Why not?"

"What's in it for me?"

"How would I know, especially since I have no idea what is in it for me?"

"Not what's in the box for me. What's in it for me if I tell you?"

"What do you want?" holding the box, shaking it by my ear.

"What do I want for telling you what's in the box, Dentine?"

"Yeah?"

If she keeps playing around, I will open this sucker up and find out for myself.

"Why don't you do that?"

"Do what?"

"Open the box, idiot?"

"Hey, "idiot" hardly rhymes."

"I give up," she fumes. "You're completely clueless to everything."

I stare at my departing adversary for a moment. A moment... before returning my attention to the box I am shaking near my ear. A moment... before re-returning my attention to my gone adversary. She just storms out? Frustrated by something, she just leaves? What was that little bit–

"You don't want to finish that thought, do you, Dampy?"

Why that... ummm. I think I better go upstairs.

Hitting the top of the stairs, something taps the cranium: dear Miss Swydni lingers downstairs. Her door begs me in. Her attitude begs to differ.

Why not go on in? We can see her progress on that "Vi" thing.

Should I? What, tell me, what should I do?

Check out the present in my hands in my room and live long enough to enjoy it! THAT is what I should do!

Who would send me a present, anyway? My birthday highlights another calendarial page. Could Kismet have sent it? Should I make out a "thank you" note?

Make out. With her. We could do it at her church.

Church? Sunday? Is today Sunday?

Open the damn present!

The present? Hold it. Better open the note first.

Note? Note: what am I doing?

If only I could stand alone in the unemployment line. Yo, Dinky?

"Conscience?"

Would you kindly open the thoughtful note on the package and repeat the same process, adapting for size differentials, on the package the note is taped to?

"Open the note? Okay. 'Accept this gift.'"

How strange. I remember hearing that line before.

Gosh. Whom from?

"Are you patronizing me, Conscience?"

Heavens, no. But could you open the present now, by chance?

"If you insist."

Yes, buddy. I do.

The present's wrapping paper wraps never more. The shirt box is not a shirt box. In fact, this package reads...

'Rosie Mano!' Give her to me!

"Rosie Mano? What is a Rosie Mano?"

Listen, instead of wasting your mouth talking, blow that beauty up and give it to me.

"You know about Rosie Mano? How?"

Statistically speaking, I "wake up" every thirty minutes when you sleep. Since you saw logs big time, nobody keeps me company – surprise, surprise. Anyway, I click the TV on and watch late night shows. Catching the snippets I can informs me that Rosie Mano is quite the polyurethane marvel. By the way, this month's phone bill will cost.

"What about Rosie Mano?"

I heard about her through adult bookstore ads and the Hormone Shopping Network.

"And you ordered her?"

No, but I prayed real hard. Gimme!

"Wait a minute. Adult bookstore? I remember something about an adult bookstore. What chapter was that?"

Dinky, think. Just one time, think. You have an unsigned note with a signature statement frommmmmm? Play along.

"Russell!"

Riiiiiiight. And who was in the adult bookstore? Think, dude.

"Russell?"

Good puppy. So whom could this note be from?

"Russell."

Good. Blow her up and gimme!

"Rosie Mano? Is this a love doll or something?"

Or something. And instead of blowing her up yourself, get that air pump behind the vacuum cleaner you never use and gimme.

"Vacuum cleaner?"

Air pump!!! Plug it in, plug Rosie up and put her in the corner. We can both watch her grow before our eye!

"Good idea."

Well, one of us has to use his head for something other than a hat rack.

Drop the conversation. Find the air pump.

I find the thing. Plug it in. Put Rosie in the corner. Plug her up. Something puzzles me about the whole situation, though. Rosie Mano? Mano? Mano?

Wow! Watch her grow!

Rosie Mano?

Are those fingernails?

Mano?

Big fingernails!

Rosie?

When will the rest of her body balloon?

Mano?

This has the makings of a big woman! Biiig woman!

Mano? Hold it! Mano is Spanish for...

There's something real familiar about that babe!

It finished growing. I cannot believe my best friend bought this for me. I stand, turning the pump off.

Rosie Mano.

Mano: Spanish for hand. Rosie: self-explanatory to men.

Rosie Mano.

Russell bought me a nicely manicured, soft, supple, clenched hand the size of a human body. And THIS was supposed to put me in the right frame of mind?

Your friend has quite a sense of humor. Can we try her?

"No! We are taking a shower."

Yo, Dinky. Just one time. A quickie.

Accept this gift? He bought me a hand. Like the two I have are broken.

He bought me a hand!

Dinky's note: the scene previously in this spot was a multi-page shower scene. But no matter how cool and futuristic singing in a holographic/virtual reality concert hall may be, a multi-page shower scene for one was just too much to... uh... never mind.

Returning to MY reality... after a few psuedo-sets, the microphone starts pulsating cold water. My cue to exit this shower gig. If only the real world... never mind.

This stage I leave is just another set, another prop symbolizing the theater called my life. Life itself is a stage where we act in character. Characters we choose to be. Hereditarily speaking, directors placed near-finite definition on our casting, pre-printing the generality our persona starts out with. Environmentally speaking, interactions in and about all worldly levels catalyst our maturing matrix. For the most part, though, we, ourselves, decide if the plot reeks of villainy or heroism. Good Other Guy or bad Other Guy.

I seem to have auditioned for supporting cast in my own existence. I got the job, too. Uncontested. Nonetheless, my comeback debut in the grander, leading role takes place tonight. It has to; otherwise, my life has no candidate eligible for the Academy Award for leading actor in a non-fictional fiction.

I just hate where my personal cotillion takes place. In fact, I totally hate everything that could transpire next.

COULD BE LAST CHAPTER

Why am I here? I hate this place. Marine Corps butterflies have overtaken my stomach. Nervousness overwhelms this wayward soul. All because of this place.

How did Russell get me here?

"Russell, h-h-how did you get me here?"

"I asked you, then I drove you."

He truly can take this situation a lot easier than me! He should! He comes here often enough to list it as a secondary residence!

"Relax, Dink. Stay with me and tonight, your problem's history."

"What problem?" responding as if this subject were new.

Russell recoils, putting his I-better-listen look on his face, which is customarily followed by him dipping his voice an octave.

"Dink, remove you butt from my car, go inside and have fun."

I hate this place.

We leave the car and walk towards the door. Russell's name bounces vocally across the evening parking lot at least four times, each time laced with more feminine horniness than the prior one.

Females drooling for my buddy.

I hate this place.

This place, Toe Goes, is, without a doubt, the hottest bar in the county. Promiscuity saturates everything. The patrons, the music, the bar glasses, even the motto suggest sex: "If you leave alone, seek counseling."

I already made a psych appointment.

At the door, Russell knocks twice and twice more. An eye slit slides open. The doorman and he briefly exchange stares before Russell whispers something in a foreign language. The door opens.

Who is this individual who doubles as my best friend?

Once inside, Russell grabs my shoulder.

"I'll help you anyway I can," he encourages, "as long as it is of no inconvenience to me."

What a swell guy.

"Whatever you want, Dink, if you want it, is twenty minutes away."

That line helps. I take a deep breath, turning to thank him.

Gone.

Did he get paged? Anyway, his comment did stilt my ego. So stilted, I venture towards the coatroom, but a mini-dress flawlessly filled collars my covet.

Yummm.

Studying her like the horny man who be me, I advance upon her, trying to gurgle something intelligent. Before word one exits my mouth, she extends her index finger, places it on my lips, visually interrogates my entire body and laughs.

A soft sweet laugh? No. That would be a giggle. She did not giggle. Instead, she reached down deep to harvest this chuckle.

Totally embarrassed, I slither away.

Strike one.

Scope the bar.

That mellow voice sounds very familiar.

Dinky, success bids itself better if you find out where you are within where you are.

Scanning my immediate area, nobody remotely acknowledges my presence.

Scope the bar, Dinky. Investigate before we donate.

"Russell," the sheep inside utters, "is that you?"

Dinky? Have you visited this place before?

"Conscience?"

Scope the bar. Find out the situations and the females.

Great! In a bar full of erotic people, I offers me the only conversation. If myself joins in, we can have a threesome.

Scope the bar.

Another example of thinking with the wrong head.

*Dinky, scope... *

"Yeah, yeah. 'Scope the bar.'"

Toe Goes does grant ample scoping opportunities, housing four bartending stations, three good-sized dance floors on two levels and a partridge...

Uh uh. Not going there.

Anyway, the two "partying" dance floors reside on the first level. The top level has the "courting" dance floor, for people wanting more intimate, getting-to-know-you, vertical liaisons after first meeting down below.

Thirty minutes later at street level, the scoping yields bad luck. Meat factories grind less than the people on the dance floors.

Me? I scope.

Ten minutes later, strike two. A transvestite sporting a huge Adam's apple. For future references, multi-sexual shuns hurt more than heterosexual shuns. Homosexual shuns are foreign to me, but the night is still young.

Thirty more minutes later, very little luck. An interesting prospect developed, but I lost my nerve and sit at a safe distance.

Ah, a woman in close proximity captivates me, sitting on that barstool, bumping on every beat. I want her supreme body.

Me, too. Go for it!

Why not? What else could happen? I hijack some confidence and approach her. Swimming through the gyrating crowd, I split our distance when she looks up. I freeze.

Go for it, Dinky!

"Leavemealone!!!"

The music reduces our distance more. We lock eyes. Ohhhhh, yeah! She irrefutably craves some "Dinky dejour."

The music bumps heavier. I buoy at her port of joll. She licks her moist, ruby lips slowly and very suggestively.

Yes!

Without a word, I grab her hand, help [or possibly yank] her up and start for the dance floor. It took longer than 20 minutes, but success is mine.

Deep amongst the euphonious re-production plant, the dance floor, I notice a clearing to lead her to. Abruptly, my conquest crushes my hand.

Hey, baby. Crush me.

Turning my head to question her actions, a firm slap halts my cranial rotation. She then withdraws her hand and screams...

"No!"

No? She said no? And not just no. She said, "No!" I know. I heard. Everybody heard.

Now normally, "no" gathers meager attention from anyone outside of the immediate conversation. But let me receive that word in a loud, crowded, orgy-casino-of-a-bar and you suddenly hear crickets.

Dancers stop grinding. Waitresses stop waiting. The deejay stops mixing. Everyone stops... and looks at me. The Other Guy.

This incident means much more than strike three. The lunchroom massacre makes a tame comparison. This incident ends the inning, the game, all post-game interviews and closes the stadium for the season.

The Other Guy. I hate him. Why Pops passed this disease on torments me more than actually having it.

Werewolf? Oh yeah. Easily, a DNA malfunction men should readily inflict on the bearer of their loins.

Insanity? Another good gene-distorter any man-child would emulate just so they can mimic their father. At least a lifetime's supply of rubber rooms comes with the package.

What else? Monstrous stupidity, no body hair, bigbutticus, anything but The Other Guy.

>>Sigh<<

Okay, okay, okay. I feel okay, now. Like somebody cares. I even caught Conscience wanting to ooze out the front door in the heat of the fiasco.

During the appreciation speech of my peculiarity, kinly speaking, I maneuvered a path to the bathroom. While partaking that eternal mile, many people expressed grave concern over my condition. Not exactly the humility recently bestowed, but how I maintained control of my motor reflexes after receiving a near-fatal blow.

And the deejay? He was nice. He dedicated a special song over the sound system: "This song goes out to the brave brother who brunted forbiddance from that beauty."

Ahhh, thank you, Mr. Mixmaster.

In the restroom, standing over the sink, someone loses his dinner in the stall directly behind me. Despite hurling huge, splashing chunks into the porcelain prayer stand, he can still find fun. Dump in enough breath mints to resemble an extra set of teeth and tally ho, tally whore.

>>Sigh<<

Placing my attention at the person in the mirror before me reveals a pathetic sight. How long will he/I let the water splash in the sink and out onto his crouch area, thus giving him/me the pissed-in-his-pants look?

The Other Guy. Poster child for Murphy's Law.

If only The Other Guy would leave my love life alone – or allow a love life, period – I could be happy. No one should have the difficulties and inept circumstances the ruler of my destinies believed my being lacked. Annnd I could stand here and drown Conscience, were it here. I could. Who cares what happens to me? In fifty years, who will mention tonight?

Only everybody and their grandchildren.

Grandchildren. Heh. No chance for me to grab the "grampa" title. No chance for me to grab the "dad" title. I run from the practice sessions.

Wah.

"I thought you left."

Yeah. Right. Kill the pity party. Nobody RSVPs them and even fewer people show up. Shuck the b.s., turn off the faucet, dry me and get to scoping. We desperately need experience when we stop running from Destiny.

"Kismet."

Whoever. This is Toe Goes, dude. We look good. We have sympathy. Use it on a blonde and churn, baby, churn.

For once, Conscience has a point, albeit primal. Scooping deep inside myself for the infinitesimal amount of remaining confidence, I stride to the automatic hand dryer.

Broken. A forecast of things to come? Maybe. Maybe The Other Guy saying he lives within without my concern.

Come on! Get a grip! The drier is broken. Untuck your shirt and find that blonde!

Untucked, I reach the exit and reach for the door handle. Opening the door with, duh, confidence, I move forward through the doorway and notice something familiar overhead.

Swydni's logo. She puts it on all of her inventions. What did Brainhead Barbie invent that would be in a bar?

H-h-h-hold it! The thing in her lab from the third chapter. Damn.

Transcending, yet available as a practical joke, a socially significant device for our sexually dangerous times erupts. The technology that created such a situation – such a device – eludes me. What does not elude me is the bells, the whistles and the pulsating red light that undoubtedly carries the infra-red beam that triggered this device after scanning yours truly. Hindsightingly speaking, the technology that created such a device does not elude, after all: The "SM1 Wall-Mounted Vi" is the "SM1 Wall-Mounted Virgin Detector."

Virgin.

V-i-r-g-i-n. Or to spell it another way [cue that really old kid show sign-off song]:

D-i-n. In big trouble.

k plus y. Why? The Other Guy.

I. M. A. Q-tip!

"Thank you. Thank you," appreciating my large, unwanted audience. "Yes, this detector removes all doubt from everyone present – and the people you will tell – that I am a virgin. Thank you, one and all, and good night."

Grrr.

"Time to go, Conscience?"

After you.

Next stop: coatroom.

Going through the commenting crowd and for my coat, my first "strike" in the mini-dress flawlessly filled remains where we parted. She tries to stop me, bringing her right index finger lip-high. My index finger, along with the rest of my hand, contemplates smacking her, lip-high.

Yeah, I wanted to slap her. I wanted to slap her hard. I also did not want to chance being a Tae Kwon Do practice dummy, again.

Slithering past, I grab my coat and put it on on my way out. It feels snug. No wonder... I grabbed a woman's coat.

So what. Keep going.

On the street, walking again, I want nothing more than to be at home. If luck prevails, Pops' voice can split a tooth this time. So what. I welcome it. That and Mom's cooking. Hunger doest possess this persona much like Poltergeist.

As if driven by a psychic network wannabe, here comes Mobile Mozzarella, the pizza shop on wheels. Great. My dinner had to be paid for anyway, might as well eat something that keeps me out of pediatrics.

Mobile Mozzarella. Thick crust, gooey cheese, extra sauce, pork toppings and he drove right past me.

Was there a little redhead girl in the passenger seat? A little redhead girl who threw her sucker at me?

Hey! A sucker? On the sidewalk? Am I that hungry?

>>Krunch<<

Several blocks later, nothing else perturbs my walk home. Thirty minutes and no afflictions, not even a stray arrow.

>>Thwip<<

I stand corrected. Parted my hair nicely, too.

Minutes later, I near home. Home. Tonight's humiliations make home feel like... like... home. A real home, not like mine.

Suddenly, a sensation. A strange awareness of my surroundings suggests something lurks terribly close. Something, or someone, awful.

On average, spotlights tend to arouse a foreboding insight of near-future punishment. There is absolutely no reason to guess what happens next, because I am... you know... him.

A police car houses the spotlight, of course. This particular police car has extra heavy duty air shocks, because behind the wheel rests Officer Hazel. Of course.

Another typical night chaperoning another typical day.

The feet keep moving. If I make it to the next house, I can sprint across the street, run behind the Elmers' house, vault over the fence and Hazel will be history.

Glancing over my shoulder for her exact location, the bright light blinds me. No matter, I know this neighborhood like the back of my hand.

My heart races. Sweat pops out of my forehead like overripe pimples. Gas flubulates my buttocks. I can make myyy mooooooooooove, now!

Exploding off the sidewalk, mini fires smolder where these loafers once stood. Freedom calls out like a long lost lover. For once, things are going my...

"Ummmph!"

True. I know this neighborhood like the back of my hand and this Subaru that has me as a hood ornament does not belong here. Remarkably, though, pain has yet to surface.

Uh oh. Spoke too soon.

Annnd here it comes. Excruciating. Nothing less than the best, but I need more. The driver must screech to a dramatic stop, thus, launching me from his bumper and rolling me like a rag doll on the pavement. If he stops too quickly, my exposed flesh cannot possibly collect the broken glass sparkling up ahead.

Any moment, folks.

Finally. He stops. I go, roll, collect and stop, by force, under a familiar car tire. A car door opens. Out walks Officer Hazel. Somehow, she had slipped my mind.

She slimes over [to] me, placing her feet near the top of my head. Severe injuries guarantee my present reclining position in the street. Looking up at her, I undeniably appreciate the fact she does not wear skirts.

She lurks at me. She then crotches down and softly sings in my ear...

"Tonight, you're mine. Completely!"

Yearning all night, because of and for, Kismet, along came fate minus the "e".

The mere thought of horizontally exercising with a person who has armpits thicker than rain forests regurgitates my guts.

I scream, finding no success. The Subaru took my lips.

Summing up my current situation, there bequeaths a lone possibility. Mustering all of my remaining strength, I look my sexecutioner in the eyes and irk, "Do me. Then take me..."

SHOULD BE THE LAST CHAPTER

"...home?"

What the...? Where the heck am I? Something tells me...

No. Impossible. Everything equates, though. Granted, I have major difficulties adding two plus two, but two minus two? It always equals Ground Zero.

This place resembles Ground Zero. Trust me, with my life's experiences, I know Ground Zero. Question is: why am I here?

No, the questions are: why am I here, how did I get here and, most importantly, what is the here?

The relative thing about Ground Zero is that it has been used for some type of explosive testing. In some cases, it will be used again.

The vastly charred ground reminds me of the ceiling in the kitchen. Concentric circles, except devoid of color. Was one of Mom's hot-n-spicy taco quiches the result of this urban expansion?

Vast nothingness. Towers of smoke where towers of steel and concrete did stand, assuming I stand in what could have been my kitchen. Surveying the landscape, an annoying, loquacious breeze companions me.

"Richarrrrrrd, dinnnner'ssss rrrrrready."

Ooooooo-kay! Winds and breezes can make some frightening noises, but that was down-right terrifying!

"Richarrrrrrd."

"Mom?"

"Yesss. Richarrrrrrd, commmme eeaaaat."

I would rather pass. You can interpret that anyway you want.

"Arrrrrre yyooouuuu commmmming, Richarrrrrrd?"

"Did you cook the feast, mother of the wind?"

"Yessssssssssss, Richarrrrrd."

"Nooooooooooo."

>>skkrmmmmbrkrk-BOOM<<

Uh huh.

Big, bombastic clap, that one was. Filled the air. Motivated it almost. Not to create a gush or a breeze, mind you, or any wind manifestation. Atmospheric pressure shifted, though, almost down to the molecular level.

How would I know what happens at the molecular level? Is something adding up? The two's? Where are the two's?

Anyway, no wind pours about, but a sucking sound, an actual sound, builds. An angry draw builds and spreads. Builds and festers. It crosses its limited audio dimension into its cousin's realm of solid. Surrounding colors, not noticed prior, are swept to a gathering source. A source unrevealed. Much noise, much movement, yet, no wind.

What happened? What is happening?

My face mirrors my inclinations. Burying it in my hands to protect it, the sound grows. My ears must also double as visage assembler, because the only things I care to actually see are the lifelines on my palms.

Shrinking lifelines.

The draft-substantive pulls harder. Why am I unmoved? Why do I sense vibratic substance? Why do I...?

It stopped. No sounds. No interpreted moving. No nothing.

My hands drop to my side. Eyelids open. Now, where am I?

>>snif<<

Kansas? Hold it. Hold it. Hold it. Hold it. Hold it!!! Kansas?

Kansas! Dorothy! Kansas! I hated that dog! Kansas! Dreaming! I am dreaming!

Sigh of relief? Definitely!

Mr./Ms. Reader? Are you lost? Well, apparently the wormhole in my unconscious subconscious took me from ground zero to a prairie. No little house, but a prairie nonetheless. Of course, in a prairie without the little house, there has to be wheat. As far as the eyes can see. Pre-bread. Would you think Kansas at this point?

Okay, how about the powder blue skies? Kansas?

Okay, how about the billowing, floating, flowing, cottony rolls of toilet paper, i.e., clouds? Hopefully that one directly overhead is a thundercloud. Either that or some angel cleaned his/her awfully big buttocks.

Kansas? Not yet? Okay, smell this page.

Yep! Did for me, too!

>>Nok<<

Knock? First, I get sucked from who knows where to who cares where and then I get a knock?

>>Nok<< >>Nok<<

Knock? Knock? Does somebody want to come into my dream?

>>Nok<< >>Nok<<

"Come in. Come to Kansas."

>>Nok<< >>Nok<<

"Come in!"

You know, this place is pretty nice. As I currently scope around, I think I can see how somebody could settle down here. Peaceful, hypnotic...

>>Nok<<

120

"Come! In!"

"Dinkiempht."

The clouds? They talk? Truly a dream.

Opening my arms for a hearty welcome, I eagerly await the femininity that tried to carry my name my way.

Holllllllllllld it! A woman calling my name? A woman calling me? A woman wants my attention? Heaven wants to send me an angel!

Despite semi-consciousness, this surreal could be real! I could get real busy! I just hope the wheat understands my quest for piece on earth.

"Wake up, Dorky."

There seems to be a lot more angels up there with big buttocks, all of the sudden.

"Wake up! Wake up!"

"In a minute."

>>Sssssssssssscht-POW!!!<<

"Owwwww!"

The sandman sure whacked that eviction notice with a vengeance. No. Not the sandman...

"Swydni."

"You have to wake up."

"Excuse me, missy," looking up at her. "I am in bed."

"I'm surprised you could find it in this mess."

"Be that as it may, I am in bed. I was sleeping in bed. I found it and I want to sleep in it. If you would kindly get the hell out, I will go back to sleep in the bed I found."

During my soliloquy I realized something very weird. Swydni rarely comes within an area code's distance of my room. Whatever brought her here scares me.

"Dinky," she cries softly, "it's Russell."

Swydni crying? I am still dreaming? Mom's hamburgers take how-to-be tough lessons from this girl. I hate imagining what could activate her tear ducts *and* have her call me Dinky.

Hey! She said something about Russell! Oh my God!

"Russell??? Swydni, is something wrong with Russell???"

The anxiety springs me on top of my bed, positioning myself to grab for her shoulders and shake some info from her.

She shoots me a look signifying the law I almost break: never touch her!

I forgot. Had the crime taken place, she would have reenacted an Ellie Mae/Jethro Bodine fight scene. The ones that always conclude with Ellie Mae tying Jethro in a knot and Uncle Jed coming to his rescue.

Excuse me, I drift from the topic of importance.

"What happened to Russell?" with hands in pockets.

"H-h-his mother," she whimpers, "she's..."

"Stop! Stop right there! You know how Russell's mother treats me. How can you mention that woman in my room?"

"She had a heart attack, Dumbo!"

"Dinky."

"We don't have time for this. Mrs. Russell is sick. She's at the hospital."

"So."

"So? Go see her! She's your best friend's mother."

"So."

"Go!"

"No."

"Jeeeeeeeeeeeeeeeeeeeeeeeeeed!!! Swydni! Stop!"

"You going?"

"Yeah! Yeah! Untie me!"

"Promise?"

"Only if you stop watching those rodeo wrestling matches."

"Deal. Go."

A shower, shave, costume change and scene change relocate me. To the hospital. Information desk.

"Excuse me, nurse."

Whoa. Nurse? Maybe. Man? It appears.

"Oooh, it's that big kid. How you doing widdle person? Want a sucker?"

"No," taking the initiative, "a girlfriend. Interested?"

"Say, bud," now defensive. "Men make excellent nurses."

"Yeah, right. Busy Saturday night?"

"What do you want, baby-man?"

"Awfully glad you dropped the subject, ma'am. I need some patient information on a Mrs. Russell. Her first name is... umm..."

"Room 2036A."

"Thank you. Where, umm...?"

"Past pediatrics. Take a left."

"Very funny. Wear red on Saturday."

Leaving the man in white, I cannot help but wonder how strange that last exchange went. Not the preference for blouse color, but how that [s]him knew which Mrs. Russell I meant? There must be more than one here. Better yet, how would fe/male know her room number without looking it up? Weird.

Anyway, up the elevator, past pediatrics... hold it! Why not pay Mae a visit?

Approaching the check-in desk, I notice another male nurse in Mae's stead. Definitely equal opportunity.

"Excuse me, nurse."

"It's you," this more female, male nurse perks.

"Have we met before?" which I would remember.

"No, doggonit."

"Then how... never mind. Is Mae in today?"

"She's ill. Can I help you? I really want to."

No response, just retreat. A speedy retreat.

"I'm just smashing in red," the nurse yells behind me.

Very weird.

Okay, past pediatrics, take a left. 2033. 2032. 2031. Wait a minute. The other left. 2033. 2034. 2035. 2036? 2036. Open the door.

The door opens itself. A SwydnInc. invention? No. Russell coming out.

"Hey," greeting him in the hall. "How is she?"

"Tired," he dejects. "Go on in. She'll be happy to see you."

"Yeah. Right. Where are you going?"

"She wants something to drink. Go on in."

"Alright, already!"

I re-open the door as he goes. Lightly stepping into the room, in the bed rests...

"Mae?"

She awakens.

"Dinky," straining to whisper. "Hi. Come in."

"Strange seeing you here. I came looking for Russell's mother. Russell, the guy who just left. I tried catching you in pediatrics, but they, well, that happy male nurse said you were ill. Ill. What a word. Anyway, I came in here expecting to find Mrs. Russell. Instead, I find you. Weird, huh?"

"Just like you talking this much."

"Huh? Oh, yeah. Say, uhhh, how are you? What happened?"

"Mild heart attack."

"Like Russell's mother. Talk about coincidences."

She gives me a baffled expression, much like those Russell gives me when I scorn the prominent. What two and two have I failed to add this time?

"Dink."

Ah, he returns.

"It figures," turning to him. "Of course, two of the dearest people in Carlisle would know of each other."

"Dink..."

"Quiet, Russell. Let me roll, okay? Where was I? Oh, yeah. Mae. Russell. Two dear and significant people in my life. Life is good. When did you two meet?"

"About twenty-two years ago," Russell responds.

Mae sits quietly with an unusual quirk on her face.

"We met in a hospital, pretty much like this one."

Twenty-two years? In a hospital? Pretty much like this one? I predict pain.

"C'mon, Dink, really? That's my mother."

Oh. Okay. Keep... the scream... internal. I got my two plus two and the four. It hurts.

"Your what?!!!!!!!!!!!!!!! Mother?! Maeeeeee?!!"

"Dink. Dink. Dink!"

"You sound like an elevator, Russell."

"Dink..."

"Fourth floor! Women's cosmetics, lingerie, hand guns and Kook-A-Munga!!!"

"Dink, quit screaming and get a grip on yourself!"

"Get a grip on myself?!!! Get a grip on myself?!"

Hmmm.

"I live next door to you for years! Years! And Mae?! I lived next to you for... the same amount of years! Why am I now finding out this... this... this this!"

"Because you're dumb sometimes, Dink?"

"Dumb?! Me, dumb?!"

"And blind."

"Blind?! Me, blind?!"

"Will you calm down? You're scaring Apocalypse."

"From YOUR HOUSE??!!!"

"No, from behind you. Calm down."

"B-behind me?"

I turn to look at it. Why? I could have taken Russell's word for it. He never lies. No. He just never tells me who is mother is!

"How could you...?"

Do not disturb the grieving dog. The grieving dog in a hospital. Walk to my friend and loudly whisper to him, instead. Yeah, yeah. Walk to him.

"How could you do this to me, Russell? How could you keep a secret this big from me? Your best friend? Mae? How could you? I thought I was your friend."

"Dinky," she strains, "no, Richard, no, Dopey..."

"Not funny!"

"Dinky. We tried to tell you. Years ago. But as hurt as you are, believe me when I say, it doesn't compare."

"Dink," putting his hand on my shoulder, like he was a friend. "Dink, you better leave. We're all just getting upset here. I'll talk to you later. When Mom's up to it."

"Russ—"

"Dink," in a deathly calm voice. "We'll talk later."

"Awright," exchanging like a tough wimp.

I walk to the door, but before opening it, I glance back to see a wounded woman struggling to rest.

Why?

A reviving Apocalypse informs me to figure this out at a later date... in a safer place.

I make my way out of the hospital. Countdown the room numbers, take a right into...

No, please.

"See ya Saturdayyyy," he sings. "I'll wear enough red to be a fire engine."

What did Mom say about loving and losing?

No. No way.

Hmmmm.

No!

Hmmmm.

NO!

Elevator.

Disembarking from the elevator, I try to sneak past the other male nurse. The more masculine male nurse. Or, at least, I try to sneak by.

"Got a date, huh, baby-man?"

Walk. Keep on walking. Walking onto the streets, but to where? Where can I go? A question that could apply to more than my feet. Where am I going? Why am I so confused? I mean, this is quite a simple matter.

A woman whom I met, whom I have not lusted after. A good friend, too. No, correction: was a good friend. A good female friend who just happens to be the woman I have loathed for years. The same woman who chews cigars. The same woman whose voice I had not heard, or, at least, I thought I had not heard.

Where am I going? Hold it. I can get there faster.

"Taxi!"

One pulls up. I get in.

"Twenty-four-o-five, please."

As the meter runs, I try to understand this situation. I have lived next door to a remarkable woman for eight years. My best friend's mother.

"Heh. My best friend. I question that."

"Yo, mack, you jaw'n to yourself?"

Forgot I was thinking loud enough to get an audience.

"Yeah, driver. I guess I was."

"Call me Lewis."

"Yeah, Lewis. I guess I was."

"What about?"

"Life."

"What about it?"

"Good question. What about it? Take for example, I recently found..."

"Kid. I've been haulin' people for years. Upper class, lower class, but no middle class, cuz that's been done away with."

"You got a point, Lewis?"

"Yeah. Somethin' confuses you, step back to proceed, if'n you have to. Do something. Don't let it kill you. If something throws you for a loop, do the loop and keep on going."

"Is that all?"

"No, twenty-four-o-five."

"You made your point, Lewis. How long before we get there?"

"We're there. Pay up."

"How much?"

"Twenty-four-o-five."

I pull out a twenty and a five, paying as I get out, motioning him to keep the change. The cab ride may have seemed short, but getting caught up in my thoughts speedwinds all clocks.

"Hey, kid, don't spend too much time trying to understand. Whatever bothers you today will only wait for you with its brother tomorrow. If you let it."

Out of the cab. Back on the courts. The courts. Life made simple. Three-to-five persons making up one of the two teams fighting over an air-filled ball of bounce. One team battles to put the ball through a circular wire of thick metal with strings hanging from it. The other team fights to stop that from happening. That is, until they possess the rubber rock. Then they dare to do what the first team did, but the first team blocks their efforts like the second team tried to thwart the first team's efforts.

Life made simple.

Why do I even come here as often as I do? Why do I come here, period? Granted, I can play basketball, but in a city this size, there are more courts than Twenty-four-o-five. Perhaps my future psychiatrist will suggest I visit this locale, because Pops has hooped a few homies in this neck of the hoods and perhaps my desires to have my father be a substantial influence in my life, although, the current standings in our current relationship equates to me supplementing my recurring stops at his former joy-lodgings for his actual parent/child non-correlation.

Puh-leeze. And that was a really long sentence.

Uh oh. Rebound to reality, where things just got unsimple.

I absolutely refuse understand those two. The money they make, you would think Eugene and Lorenzo might find more constructive uses for their time. Do they, though?

No. With them, their time is best utilized altercating, debating, disputing and arguing. In this case, "who fouled who?"

>>BLAMMM<<

Oooo, technical! It was so destined to end up like this.

>>BLAMMM<<

The sound echoes. Time stands still. Or better yet, time changes its distance. Reality goes slow motion. People slowly move away from the confrontation scene. A second is a minute.

>>BLAMMM<<

126

Two guys competing for a lifetime. Someone's lifetime may have just run out.

>>BLAMMM<<

Still echoing, over and over and over.

Eugene falls ever so slowly. A crimson stain near the heart ends a stupid, continuous competition. Hard to tell if Lorenzo feels more remorse than Eugene does pain. Why is he taking so long to fall?

Maybe I can help. Help what? Who knows?

>>BLAMMM<<

Eugene reaches up. Still slow motion. He reaches up for Lorenzo's belt, bringing the gunman down over him.

What can I do?

"Lo-Loren- >>kof<< Lorenzo. Really?"

Perplexity floods Lorenzo's face. The simple question made sense. It makes sense. A lot more sense than all those years of fighting.

And just like that, Eugene's body quits and drops.

>>BLAMMM<<

Home. My room. Sitting on the bed I easily found after cleaning my room. I stare out of the funny window.

Cleaned my room? Funnier than the window, one would think.

I changed locations, but the echo continues.

Why? Why did what happened happen? Life gone for nothing. For competition? Man-made thunder spitting lead rain that terminates instead of replenishing?

What happens to Lorenzo now? What happens to Eugene? What happens, period?

Really?

"Conscience?"

Who else?

"Please. Not now."

If not now, when? Really?

"Really WHAT?!"

Albeit, melodramatic, those hams provided an excellent lesson.

"The point, please."

One unfortunate soul is headed to the afterlife. The other, the hard life. With all they had going for them – with all they had – they have nothing.

"The point? Sometime this year, please?"

What about your life?

"What about it?"

If something stupid or unexpected happened to you, you would have less to show for yourself than those dummies, although, you have more.

"More?"

More.

127

"More what?"

You have more.

"What do I do with this... more?"

Fix yourself for one.

"How?"

One step at a time.

"That really helps a whole lot."

Stop being facetious.

"Suggest something pertinent, dammit!"

You run this body! You figure it out!

Dead silence, which should be the case when talking to yourself. Excuse the poor pun.

"Okay, okay, okay. Where do I start?"

At home.

"I am home!"

That means no travel time, eh?

"Please?"

Think about it. Are you or are you not a bright... boy?

Point taken.

Pops'. His den. His door, to be precise. I should knock.

"Whudda ya want, boy?"

Oh-kay.

"Pops? Can we talk?"

"I know what'cha want and the answer's 'no!'"

"But Pops..."

"No! What part of that word don't you get?!"

"We need to talk."

"This ain't the Brady Bunch. When you wake up tomorrow, it's not to another thirty-minute episode, unless that stuff Swydni's been spoutin' 'bout's true. Y'know, about your life being a book? By the way," he now allures, "make sure you gotta good-lookin' actor depicting me."

"Uh," puh-leeze, "that would be in the movie adaptation, Pops. An audiobook was done, though."

"Whatever. Anyhow, since I ain't never, no, never, not gonna perm my hair or wear bell bottoms again, you kin just ferget about having that sugar-coated father/son relationship thing."

"Pops? Can we talk?"

"Do I have ta see you?"

"Yeah."

"No."

"Why?"

The den door opens. He moves quick-n-quiet when he wants to. Should I be more surprise that he opened the door or that he approached it undetected?

His mass stands before me.

"I heard about yur friends. Intelligent idiots, those two. Were you there?"

"How did you...?"

"I'm Pops."

And more haunting than Mom.

"You saw the situation, didn'cha, boy? Found out how short life is and you wanna right the wrongs before you punch yur time card."

"Well, if you put it that way, Pops."

"I did and I don't."

"What?"

"I don't want any part of yur family mending. You cain't put make-up on twenty-year scars, boy."

"Somebody has to start somewhere."

He squints. "Keep body limp" crosses my mind as frightful moments elapse before he... before he shrugs... and lumbers back to his chair?

"Y'know, when you was a pup, I wanted too hard to be yur father and yur friend. You couldn't tell the difference. You always saw one side of a situation at a time. That was yur biggest problem. And it prompted me to back step a bit. Drop the friend. Enforce the father."

"Be..." now at the door, "my friend."

"Teach what I know," he paternals. "How I lived."

"How could I picture you with a prior life? You were grown when we met."

"And that made you think the twenty-something generation corners the market on pre-AARP living?"

His demeanor is no longer fatherly, yet my father, nonetheless.

"I went through the same shinalo fertilizing yur life. Who do you think broke in Officer Hazel?"

Whoa. Body language punctuated that thought, too.

"Police academy. That's where I met her, and not those asinine sequels posing as cinema, either. We went through basic together. She convinced me to go semi-pro."

A nostalgic mien graces Pops' intonations.

"Cadet Hazel LeFévre," abruptly returning to irate. "I thought football would be easier than another date with her. So yeah, I know how you live. I've definitely been in..."

"My high heel shoes, Pops?"

"Just what I mean about you, boy."

He thinks I did that on purpose.

I did.

"Every dawn," he sighs, "I lose a bit more of my positive aura. My body tells itself to redirect the energies from the good stuff: wife, family, home, health. Does it happen? Nah! Instead, another layer of good fortune sheds off me like one'a those Russian matryioshka dolls. Yeah, boy," he says standing and heading towards the nearest wall, "I know how you live."

Never has he looked this vulnerable. Forgetting any meaning or possible purpose to his childhood experiences, my focus turns to the shallow surface appearance of his child rearing. Of me and how his rearing fosters thoughts of revenge.

Revenge that offers itself as it seldom has before.

Did I have another reason for coming down here? No matter. Revenge matters.

Matters?

Anyway, being the son I am, revenge shall soon accommodate a party of one. I enter his den, walk up on him and get ready to play garçon.

"Well, Oscar, I thought your gene pool had more chlorine than substantial DNA, but..."

He spins at me, spoiling the coup de grace. We stand there, face-to-face, without him actually looking at me. For a moment, though, he did. Nearly scared my bladder dry.

But now, his attention seems to span back along the time stream. His soul's windows illustrate, for my observance, his childhood. Actions and misactions extraordinarily similar to experiences I suffered – the only difference being the overabundance of bad fashion and even worse hairdos, coincidentally, on the verge of a rebound.

The scenes mature. Pops' post-teenaged version embarks on an existence with conquest and joy. A joy peaking with the introduction of Kath E Key. Soon followed by their first aqua eros.

Tastefully picturing the youthful Mom and Pops doing what comes naturally while in nature's shower appears romantic, even while remembering this particular film's actors. Soon their fondness gets a different emergence: pulsating red lights. And the way they hastily grope for their clothing means those lights top the police vehicle of one Officer Hazel. An angry Officer Hazel, who attempts to strangle Mom, only to get pummeled by Mom's skillet key chain.

The panorama fast-forwards to another pinnacle. In a hospital? Wait. In his arms. His face simulcasts the euphoria his cinematic version manifests. The arrival of a lifelong dream. A man-child. A compatible man-child.

Me?

He blinks, drawing the curtain on the show. Turning away, his humbled demeanor delivers the final blow:

"You did get the best of me... son."

He slumps out of his den, leaving me very much alone.

Damn.

The only thing worse than being alone at times like this, is being alone with your thoughts. Thoughts of stupidity striking once and boomeranging to strike again. Harder.

The spotlight of shame showcases one. No amount of root beer could drown this feeling, either. If only the tear transpiring down my cheek could solvent my stupidity.

I came down here for a different reason. I wish I had stuck to the game plan.

>>Skeeeeeeeee–<<

Huh? That sound? Familiar.

>>eeeeeeeeeee–<<

Very familiar. Switching from depressed to defense, I employ battle-honed hearing to pinpoint the origin. My mind cross-references its database for a visual match up.

>>eeeeeeeeeeeee<<

Hold it! I got i–

"Ummphf!"

"Y'know, son? Using this double-pump water-balloon shotgun with a heavy liquid damn near knocks a person clean near off'a page, don'cha think?

"Yeah, Pops... I agree,"

...spitting out words,

...saturated in paint,

...thickened by lead flakes.

"You can't go solving all yo' problems in a half'n hour. And since I got your attention, I wonder..."

>>cht-cht<< >>foomp<<

"ughnn."

"Yep! A second shot does the job right. Hey son, I love ya to death. And I will."

S
E
R
I
O
U
S
L
Y
?
?
?

Ummm, okay?

Pops and I may possibly be friends? Granted, guys do have that capacity: enemies-to-fist-fight-to-best-buds. Of course and right now, though, I hang upside down on a wall in his den, smothered in a liquid with strong adhesive properties, but Pops and I may have reached the bridge of congeniality.

Yippee.

Have I ever mentioned he hails from Texas? I reckon it kinda 'splains the accent, huh? I betcha he done made acquaintances with that Cy character, too. You know, the dude who owns that sto' at The Mall.

>>Sigh<<

Unsticking myself from Pops' wall ever so slowly, the smell of smoke precedes and foretells the arrival of my favorite child-rearer.

"I thought I'd find you down here, Richard. You talk to your father?"

"The lacquered evidence speaks for itself, Mom."

"Your father and I always thought of you as a good target. That's not why I'm here, though, Richard. I thought you should get this information from family."

"What information?"

"Richard, Hazel's been awfully happy today. Some people are speculating the worse."

She tilts her head down as if to deliver a rhetorical question?

"Rumor has it, Hazel's done the wild thing. You know anything about that, Richard?"

Hazel did the wild thing?! I thought it was all a dream. I mean... Ground Zero and all. Or was that Mom's cooking?

"Well, Richard?"

"Well, what?"

"The rumors, Richard?"

"Were there any witnesses?"

"Yes, Richard. Plenty. They couldn't actually identify the person under Hazel, but those with cast iron stomachs recorded it. They said Hazel had stamina."

"It was a dream, Mom. A dream. I mean," loosening myself from the sticky liquid, "who in their right mind would...?"

"Were you drunk, Richard?"

"What?!!!"

"How did you get home, Richard?"

"I... ummm..."

"Don't know? You don't know how you got home, do you, Richard?"

"What are you getting at? Ughnn."

Finally free from the wall, but now flat on my gut. Almost washboard, too, but flat on it, nonetheless.

"You alright, Richard?"

"I guess. You caaan come in here and help me."

"I'm sorry, Richard," she says motherly while staying at the doorway. "How was she?"

"Moooom."

And still I stuck.

"Neither one of you are exactly woman, Richard. Did you assume that role?"

"Moooom!"

"I wished you'd have pumped someone else, Richard. Imagine the irony: the woman who tried to take my husband, the mother of my grandchild."

"Mom!"

"Oh, Richard. The baby'll have a full head of hair on its knuckles."

"Mom!"

"Oh, Richard. I gotta tell Oscar your good news!"

Poof. She skiddies up the stairs.

The liquid fastens me even tighter to the floor. I have stop her. Stop her. I have to. Stop her. Yeah.

Actually, what I need is to stop the rain man imitation. I... need... to stop her from telling the world that...

"Moooooooooooooooooooommmmmmmmmmmm!"

LAST CHAPTER

Okay. I am in Pops' sanctuary, stuck to his floor. Mom popped in and out, talking to me about Hazel.

Why am I in this situation? What was I doing?

Really?

Oh, Eugene and Lorenzo. I remember.

I remember making amends with Swydni when I got home. At her lab door. Not a word said. It probably would have spoiled the moment.

My earlier atonement with Mom, after she picked me up at the clinic, went a long way towards forging a new home, also.

Thus, life seems renewed or, in my case, beginning. Understanding actual importance no longer seems to shroud itself. Life lives today. Live it simple. Live it full. Live it before I make myself throw up.

No, I have not shaved my head, launching a career of selling flowers at airports. Eugene's simple question simply showed me that the light at the end of my tunnel is not an oncoming Amtrak.

Really?

I could accomplish yon feat after I, >>th-tsssst<<, remove a certain adhesive.

I wash up, dress and prepare to leave. My clothes are nothing special. Just a light sweater/shirt, jeans and black cowboy boots.

Closing on the front door, I take the time to open it, unlike the Apocalypse situation. Thinking of which, why not pay its owner a visit, as if I really had somewhere else to go.

Making my way across the lawns, I glance down the street and see an ambulance leaving the neighborhood. Deducing ambulances in this neighborhood always have my mobile bed, and that that said vehicle leaves without me, I conclude the ambulance must have brought Mrs. Russell home.

Mrs. Russell? I forgot. Or did I?

Mrs. Russell. Do I like her now? Her affliction gives reason for even questioning such. If she were dead, human nature would make me love her. Make me think of all the good times.

And why am I motivating self-regurgitation again?

Knocking on the door, it opens. It opens? It opens without the automatic visitor system kicking in?

Anyway, going through the house, not exactly calling for anyone, I find myself... going to the kitchen? Strange. Why not go straight to Russell's room?

Walking through this house clutching another emotion more than fear [or stupidity], remorse for Mrs. Russell blankets my thoughts, my movements. Finally locating Russell in his kitchen, hesitation helps me collect whatever thoughts could help in this situation. The questionably dearest person in Carlisle astoundingly does the breakfast thing with remarkable composure.

"Russell. Hey man, please forgive me for yesterday. If..."

Hold it.

Totally visualizing the scene before me, bewilderment overcomes remorse. My best friend – never looking up at me, as usual – repeatedly dips his spoon into a bowl and retrieves... something. The only recognizable thing on the spoon is milk, I think. Common opinion suggests spoons, bowls and milk escort cereal for consumption.

The "down for the day" sign pops up on my forehead. Ill-equipped for one of our normal superficial conversations, I make an attempt at the substantial.

"Russell, what are you putting in your mouth?"

"Cereal," he volleys.

"Cereal?" I return.

"Yes. Corn flakes."

Passing shot. My serve.

"Corn flakes? Blue corn flakes?"

"Good blue corn flakes."

Another passing shot. Sustaining the current topic, I can go without scoring in this game. Besides, the continued sight of blue corn flakes will result in reservations to Upchuck City. A place I apparently convey a bona fide hankering to visit.

"These corn flakes gettin' to you? Don't worry, I'm done. There's not too many people who can stomach a lot of azure maze and matching milk."

He gets up, puts away the food and hands his bowl to the most automated automatic dishwasher in the world. It even personally thanked him for "feeding" it.

"How're you doin', Dink? Dink?"

"Huh?" pointing my attention away from Maytag 3001.

"How - are - you?"

"Fine. Yeah, fine. How are you?"

"Well... considering what's up, I'm alright."

He walks towards me. He walks past me?

"Where are you going, Russell?"

"My room."

I, uh, follow.

"Your mother," asking with undiscovered feelings, "how is she?"

"She's alright. She knew you'd be coming."

"How?"

"Could we change the subject? It hurts a little thinking about her."

On that note, upstairs we go. Nothing substantial about it. We just step. Entering his room, he stops, pauses for a moment and looks at me.

"I don't know about life anymore, Dink. Where's it going for me?"

Whoa?

"I hardly thought about losing Mom before, which is weird, losing my father'n' all. What would I do if I did?"

Again, whoa! Where is this conversation going?

"For too long, people have leaned on me and the one person I admittedly lean on was almost taken from me. Please, don't think I'm being selfish, it's just that Mom's situation hits home."

"It sounds like you question your purpose or the effort expended to stay true to it, Russell."

Thrice, whoa. Where did that bit of sage come from?

He stares at me for a moment, then walks away as if walking away from himself.

"True. On both accounts."

"Why? People have good reason for looking up to you. Your approach to life is direct and simple. People understand you, although, few really know you."

"Like you, Dink?"

"H-how did you know?"

"You sell yourself short, my friend. You think bad luck's the only one available. It makes you waste too much energy preparing for the worst. In my case, people sometimes feel... uneasy around me. They don't comprehend me well. They think I'll go ballistic one day."

He approaches me, staring at me all Norman Bates-ly.

"Why is that, Dink?"

"Umm," trying not to look guilty, "w-why is that, ummm, Russell?"

"Because I'm too freaking good to be true!"

I back away, believing he will go ballistic. Soon! Amazing, though, he was so close and never spit on me once.

"What people think of me is none of my business," he calms, pacing the room. "They can't grasp me in a moment's notice and it bothers them."

Calming less, pacing more.

"Situations happen where I've come close to compromising what's me. Too much of anything, good or bad, attracts most people. After a settlement period, they tend to shy away. So recently, I've tried diluting this town's perceptions of me. Diluting what they actually see in regards to my surface area, because they're the ones living in a remote control/microwave society."

I just look at him, unsure if he lost me in the shuffle or if he sails so far over my head that it resembles a practice target for pigeon poop.

"Remote what?"

"Remote control/microwave society. Humanity has positioned itself to think it wants everything in a hurry – regardless of the significance, like price or quality – and they refuse to get off their butts to get it. Something even odder, they don't recognize how the former seriously negates a great amount of the latter. Acquaintances, information, money, love, sex, anything. Society, as a whole, wants it. They want it now, but they don't want to work for it."

My face and mouth offer a simultaneous response:
"Huh?"

"Okay, Dink, think about this: fast food restaurants perfectly embody the microwave society. Fifteen bucks hardly pays for two burgers that may be real meat. That same fifteen at a butcher shop buys a pound of hamburger, a package of buns, a bag of chips, a two-liter bottle of pop and a pack of gum that explodes in your mouth. In this analogy, quantity and quality list as the inconsequentials. But people save time, ergo, microwave."

Pausing the conversation helps me understand him while the needle on his ballistic-o-meter swings red-ward. He never talks this much. Rarer yet, he speaks at and to me.

"And, uhm, what is the remote control, Russell?"

"Drive-ups."

"Drive-ups?"

"Drive-ups. Note: you get fast food, which isn't fast anymore. Drive-ups slow it even more, but your stay in your seat. The same thing a remote control lets you do or not do. Why not walk inside? It's guaranteed to be a lot quicker, especially around lunch time."

Red Alert!

"Go ahead, prove it!"

"Russell," trying not to soil my undies, "calm down! How about a glass of heavy water?"

"You say the strangest things sometimes, Dink," raising one eyebrow.

He probably thinks I need the nice, white dinner jacket with extra-long sleeves. The silence, although tense, lets my last statement distract him long enough to dissipate the anger. For the first time ever, Russell almost lost his cool.

Russell almost lost his cool?! And if he lost his cool, what would he make me lose?

Soon enough, a familiar Russell returns.

"People can't trust me wholeheartedly. But you – *you* – people trust."

"They should," I snap. "Why fear me when I spend enough time hurting myself?"

"You're selling yourself short again. Remember our first encounter? How I had a 'speech disorder?'"

"Like I could forget."

"'Whut's up, Dink?' Weren't those the words?"

"Right before the left cross."

"True. I needed better role models than 'Loony Toons' and that's what you gave me."

"Come again?"

"Think about it, not only do you not use contractions..."

Which explains why I say "to" too much.

"...but, you're the reason I'm me [more than you realize]. I had the foundation of a good person, but my mental super-structure lacked a few bricks. Mom..."

"Yeah! Th–"

"Don't interrupt. Mom knew you. Granted, the snowman incident worried her, but she knew you were good inside."

"Can I talk, Russell?"

"Sure."

"Then why the hell has she dogged me from day one?! And speaking of doggies, why do you two let that monster tear me into kibbles and bits?"

He pauses a moment, walks to his bed and sits down. He strikes the "Thinker's Pose" and looks up, smiling.

"Well, Dink," smiling more, "the answer for the second question is you're forgetful and stupid. Not ignorant. Stupid. Of yourself. Besides, Apocalypse needed the exercise. Mom and I decided to kill two birds with one stone."

"And my bird is?"

A hint of fear lightly spiced that question.

"Thinking. Whenever you start doing it positively about who you are – and defensively about where you are – many of your probs will be history, like Officer Hazel."

"You know about her?"

"Dink. Dinky. There aren't too many things in town I don't know about."

True.

"Put some thought into that thinking thing and your destiny gets Kismet."

This revelation stunned me more than him knowing about Hazel. My expression surely tells him that. I should ask him how he knows about her? How could he know? Then again, why bother?

"And since you forgot your question about Mom..."

How does he figure these things out?

"Are you listening?"

"Yeah. Yeah."

"About Mom, you remind her of my dad. She couldn't deal with it at first, so she hid herself from you. Eventually, her bum side became convenient at home and she kept it."

He stands and comes at me. Once there, he puts his left hand on my left shoulder. Staring at his hand and back at him, I know pain lurks somewhere, somehow.

"Dink," fashioning a grin on loan from the devil, "your day'll come. Don't rush it. Nobody solves their problems like they do on the Brady Bunch."

Hell-o!

"Russ... Russell. Russell, umm, dude? Your mother?! W-w-where is your mother?"

"You alright?

"Yeah!" No! "Why?!"

"Never mind. She's in her room. You know where it is?"

"No!Neverbeenthere!"

"Down the hall. Past the balconies. Straight ahead."

"And," attempting calm, "where is Apocalypse?"

"Don't worry."

"And what, be happy??" showing a touch of excitability. "Where is it??"

"What size dinner jacket do you wear, Dink?"

"Rus-sell!!!"

"Downstairs," chuckling breathily. "Apocalypse is downstairs in the kitchen."

"Where we were?!"

Yes, that Q was posed as I hastily run inventory on all favorable body parts.

"Don't worry. But before you leave, mind if I... pose a Q?"

"You just did, ha haaa."

"Yeah, ha ha, right," he sighs, now showing more of his familiar self. "Who do you trust?"

"Can I get back to you on that, Russell?"

"No. Who'd you incubate with?

"Huh?"

Another verbal/body language response.

"Whom did you incubate with? Who shared your incubator after you were born?"

"Nobody, I think."

"When you find nobody, trust him."

"Is this a trick conversation?"

"When you find nobody, trust him."

"Trust him? What about you?"

Silence.

"Go, Dink."

"Go? Where?"

"Down the hall. Past the balconies. Straight ahead."

"Why?"

Lost again.

"Mom's room."

"Oh, yeah. Down the hall..."

"Past the balconies. Straight ahead."

"Down the hall..."

"You want me to go with you."

"Would you?"

Down the hall we go. Past the balconies. Straight ahead. Mrs. Russell's room. I knock.

"Come in."

A rather soothing invite.

"Can I talk from here?"

Not a soothing enough invite.

"Get in there, Dink."

"No."

"Get."

"No!"

"Get!"

"Nooomph!"

He shoved me!

"You shoved me!"

"Come in."

That soothing invite again. Turning to the invitational source reveals another ridiculous room. This house! My goodness! An explanation would not do this room justice, soooo...

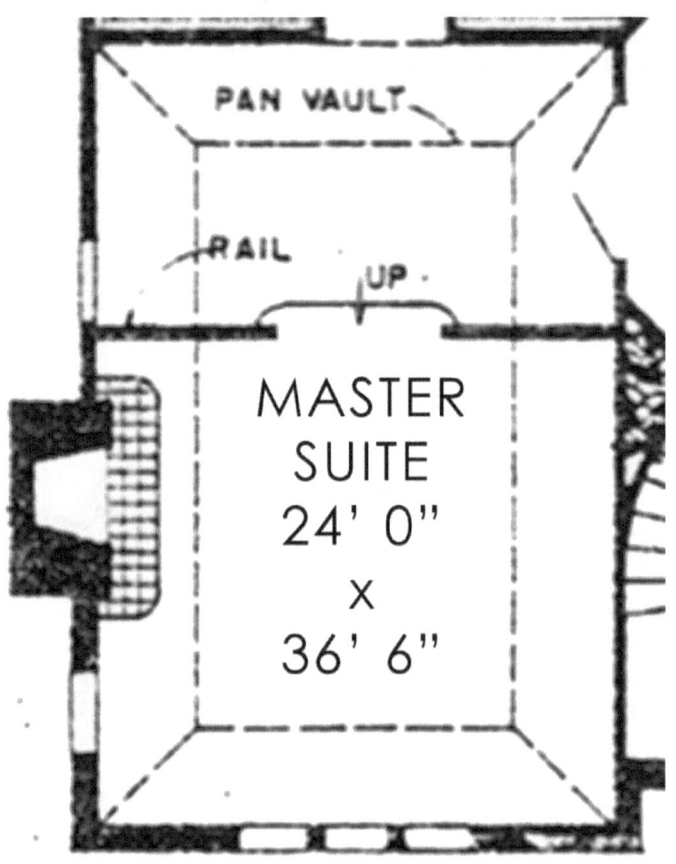

Figure 1.oh: Picture me at the double doors. Doors? Hmmm. Anyway, she is in a super-king king-size bed under the windows at the lower wall. Yes, the thick line with the gap in the middle represents rails.

What a room!

"Mrs. Russell?"

"Yes. Yes. Come."

Come, she said. Motor functions malfunction near her under the usual conditions and now, she wants me to walk the length of this... of this... continent. Maybe to hold her hand. I wonder how soft it is.

Okay, okay, the task at foot. One step at a time. Literally. Left. Right. Left. Three steps. Not even half-way to the railing. Where was I? Oh, yeah. Left, no, right. Left.

"Do your feet hurt?"

"No, ma'am. Nerves."

"Nerves?"

"Meeting you for the first time could do it. Although knowing you, or knowing about you, or knowing of you, or... you know. This room does it, too. Being as large as it is, I had to put a blueprint on the previous page."

"I beg your pardon?"

"Never mind. Anyway, you, yourself, ma'am. You look marvelous."

"Why, thank you."

"No, thank you."

Left. Right.

"Before I read the operating instructions for walking, do you mind if I really, really, really admire you."

She blushes. A hot pink blush. Although bedridden, she radiates a soft, exotic, commandeering aura. Makes me want to give a pedicure. Cooper sand nail polish. Oooooooo.

"There's no need. I'm out of that shade. Thanks, nonetheless, though."

Can every woman read my thoughts?!

"Maybe. And if walking and talking proves too difficult, I can wait for you to get over here."

"No, ma'am."

Left. Right. Left. Right.

"No need. Anyway, it seems your "bum" cosmetics hid more than your splendor. The make-up you have on now..."

"I'm not wearing any."

"Oh!" Left. "My! And what nice logs you have."

"Excuse me?"

"Your fireplace," motioning towards that section of this magniloquent loft. "Did I say something wrong?"

"A misunderstanding on my behalf. I'll probably die of old age before you get over here."

"Point taken, ma'am," picking up the pace. "Can I speak freely?"

"Be my guest."

"Well, when we met at the pediatrician's office, you treated me... with compassion."

Left. Right. Jump.

"Why there and not here?"

"I'm sure Russell told you."

"Yeah, but his explanation lacked something. Something... substantial."

"There's more to the situation. Much more! Information you should have figured out already."

"Well, this information has yet to hit me."

"It will! I can offer you something... for the moment."

She holds my hand, exuding super-duper compassion. Nice.

"Are you paying attention?"

"With tens and twenties."

"Learn how to pay attention to more than the obvious."

"Uhm, can you tell me a wee, teeny, tiny, bit more, Mrs. Russell."

"You tell me something: what sex do you think Apocalypse is?"

"What?"

"I've heard you call Apocalypse 'it' more than a few times. It's because you don't know which pronoun to address 'it' by, do you?"

"No ma'am."

This conversation changed gears without actually changing gears.

"Apocalypse rarely allows me to check out its genital area. We sort of focus on mine."

"There's more to discovering a creature than checking genitals," she says. "What sex do you think Apocalypse is?"

"Sorry, Mrs. Russell. I could not even guess."

"Then you have another surprise coming."

"Huh?"

Another two plus two? Another painful two plus two?

>>Nok<< >>Nok<<

Who the...?

"Come on in, Russell."

Oh, yeah. Who else?

He opens the door and precariously pokes his head in. Almost asking his mother a silent question.

"How's he doing, Mom?"

Somehow, this verbal Q transmits on communicative levels transcending above, beyond and on the norm.

"He's waking up," she says witnessing me. "You," talking to me, "you have a lot of magnificence to unearth. Listen to yourself. Really listen. In due time, your problems'll figure themselves out."

I just look at her. I think I love her.

"At first, you overfed my suspicions, young man. Then, later on, my suspicions faded as I had hoped your insecurities would. Tell me, what do people call you?"

"We went through this already, Mrs. Russell."

"You carry too many internal conflicts. Because of such, you answer every name with the same vigor. More so with Swydni. Do right for and of yourself. If you do right, right does you."

"Russell says that."

" ."

Attempting to respond almost in kind, Mrs. Russell – sensing my inability for such – extends her index finger and places it on my lips. Almost, like, signaling me to truly rejoinder from the heart.

I understand.

"We shall see... Dinky."

Pause.

Not exactly feeling the "E.S.Please Leave" signal, it seems the intelligent thing to do. As I smile at my new, new friend, she withdraws her finger. I take my exit, stage left.

Okay, I have a few pages left of my life open to you, Mr./Ms. Reader, and yet, the plot has not occurred. Remember in The Following Chapter, and I quote:

I go on record as admitting virginity. This lists as the
underlying main plot. Not the virginity itself, but ridding
myself of it. About time, you ask? Why admit it now, so
freely, you ask? Why not now, I ask! Few things happen with
consideration to calendars and convenience. Women,
periodically speaking, understand one and the other
intrinsically. Besides, one's first sex is the main plot in almost
everybody's life. Whether you admit it or not, whether it
underlies your intended actions or not, sex does more than sell.

Well, if you also remember the Foreword – which you were asked to read – you may recall life has no real plot. No, correction: my life has no real plot. If you were looking for a book with a plot, disappointment blocks your search. Yeah, that sounds about right.

Anyway, perhaps the most important thing I have realized is things, or situations, always happen quickly and that the obvious is not so obvious to me. A point Pops recently tried to tell me. The Russells finally did. Could this be my real plot, as well as someone's you know and love?

I also admit to wearing glasses so rose-colored they are scented. Call it the "two plus two" syndrome. I still have the feeling, though, that my glasses cannot come off for a bit to come. I still have more pages to go. Maybe, I can take off the glasses and fulfill the plot I wanted. The one I really wanted.

Descending the stairway, I hear extra footsteps, yet, cannot figure out where from.

Did we not just cover this?

I stop. The footsteps do not. Turning towards the source reveals the force behind many of my fears:

"H-h-hi, Apocalypse."

No. Remember.

"Hello, Apocalypse."

As I approach and ease around this pooch, why not pose a Q?

"Can I check your sex?" I ask, bending and reaching for parts private.

"Grrrraump," it snaps.

"Okay," springing back. "That sounded like a 'no.'"

Maybe I tried to overcome fears too fast. Calm down. Slack the tension. Assume and imply influence.

"Hey, buddy, want some hash?

"Haroomf."

"Cool. That we can do."

And off to the kitchen we go.

Who would believe mere hours ago, the only food I had to offer this dog was butt steaks. Entering the futuristic kitchen, Apocalypse instructs me where the hash, the can opener and the bowls are and how to operate the microwave. At least, I think it resembles a microwave. Anyway, the food cooks and it smells good.

Real good!

"Apocalypse, where are the forks."

"Hroomf?"

"The forks? Where are the forks?"

"Rrrrhaie?"

"Why? Because this hash smells good. I want some."

"Grrrrrrrrrrr."

"Listen. Are we, or are we not, buddies? Buddies share. Do you understand? Buddies share."

"Grrrrrrrrrrrr."

"Apocalypse! When you talk to me, look me in the eyes! Look me in... Oh! Spit!"

"Grrrrrrrrrrrr."

Buttonfly bulls-eye.

"Haahrrammmph."

Missed. Barely. Again.

"P-tui."

Gone!

Heading straight for the front door, I see Russell leaning on the kitchen entranceway.

"Dink, I came down here to settle our, or my, last problem. But I see you've got greater concerns right now, huh?"

"Yeah," screaming and streaking. "What did I do? Why is Apocalypse mad?"

"Dogs don't like to share their food. That's why."

"Okay, okay, I admit the mistake. Call it off."

"Sorry, dude. No can do. Anything else, maybe. But not food."

With Russell being absolutely no help, I shoot past him with Apocalypse hot on my heels. In fact, I feel its hot breath on my heels. It feels like a thermal foot soother.

Nice.

Returning the thought processor to the task at hand, I recall how the ivory/wood door posed little obstruction. This new door has no chance of survival. If Apocalypse could slow a touch... naww, skip it. Go through the door.

Since this scene is a rerun, meet me in the foyer.

What took you so long?!! No time for a diagnostic, thanks to you! Initiate countdown!

Three

"Rrrrrroo."

Huh?

>>PWANG<<

"Uhhhnnnn."

That sound. Where...? Why... why is it so dark?

Heaven. Could our hero's last "wood" journey land him in the check-in lobby of Hotel Heaven? Not exactly. The symphonic enchantment, lightly endowed with an awesome bass riff, may confuse the uninformed. The Other Guy? He just experienced a severe comatose.

Author?

Shut up.

A pinhole of light pricks the null. Within the spark of hope, a form. Shapeless. Fuzzy borders. Growing distinct.

Human? Nooo. Hu-woman! And familiar!

You know, The Other Guy deserves a break. If he suppresses the pain, he gets it.

Pain? What pain?

Shut uuup.

The beautiful form draws near. Garbled, filtered words seemingly originate from her.

"Wuh ayh strwan dur."

Yeah. Whatever.

The form within the pinhole within the null reaches out... to him? Is this a dream? Where did those chimes come from? Does it matter? Does he have the strength to interact? Let's see.

"Kithmeh?"

He tried, but the form coiled.

147

So, as the intelligent amongst you readers ponder the obvious, Dinky's previously mentioned pain swells.

"Ruaahh–"

>>TH'MOK<<

He's rebuffed. Spewed out by his inanimate captor. Grounded. Slowly... slowly he regains the semblance of awareness.

Mrs. Russell... bought... a solid metal door? She bought a solid metal door!

Being just so slight of consciousness, he fails to recognize my presence. Imagine his surprise to discover himself flat on his back, incapacitated, yet witnessing an extraordinary act.

"Apocalypse. Why are you putting on that bib? How are you putting on that bib???"

On cue, we leave our hero at this most opportune time to venture elsewhere. To the opposite side of the great metal entranceway.

Homina. Homina.

Ahem, excuse me.

On the opposite side of the great metal entranceway, a sweet aromatic swims on the wind, saturating the air with a scent potpourri envies. The sun, poignantly yellow, summons.

You answer.

Soaring upward and onward, an occasional glimpse back leaves a permanent impression of the hindsight the land showcases. Reeling at how closely Earth's and mankind's spirits interrelate, our atmospheric apex draws near.

The orb below opens its history, imparting grand impressions onto previously societal-blinded eyes. Since its birth, Sol's third child has supported many wars, many battles, many conflicts. Man has encountered opponents of intangibility, opponents of himself, opponents of beasts.

One such war currently takes place: man v. beast. A conflict so heavily dominated by man, Vegas stopped giving odds. A battle man rarely – rarely – loses! Whether sport or survival, the contest between man and beast almost always ends with man standing.

"Apocalypse... NOOOOOOOOOOOOOOOOO!!!!!!"

Not this time.

ummm...

EPILOGUE

>>Bing bong<<

"Apocalypse. Leave Dink alone."

"R-Russell?"

>>Bing bong<<

"Shhhh," kneeling beside me. "Apocalypse simply wanted to test the new you."

The smile drops. For some reason, Russell slides to serious. Before he says whatever, the reshaped metal door opens, unveiling my angel. My plot.

"Kismet?! You were in my dream. I tried to apologize for..."

"You weren't dreaming," she chills. "Your head was in the peephole."

"Can I help you with something, Ms. Kirk?"

Russell's demeanor. What am I missing?

"There's a discrepancy in your last billing. If you help me with our friend, we can consider the matter paid-in-full."

"What am I to you people, loose change?"

Without another word said, they prop me to my feet. As they do, I watch them eye each other. Eerie and... familiar. Russell steps back. I feel flipped.

"C'mon, Dinky."

Not exactly reading her, I foresee the future.

Turning to the releasing Russell, he gives me an expression which suggests going with her. Maybe he sees the future, too. And before I forget...

"Russell? From now on, call me Dinky."

Feeling confident and very proud, I grab my supporting femme, letting her understand she has me for the duration with no fear of finishing by herself. I kiss her and kiss up.

She smiles. A fiendish smile at that. Am I ready?

Yes, we are!

149

Yeah. I am ready. I want this. I want this. I want this. If I say it enough, I may convince myself that I want this. I want...

"Whulp!"

Her snatching me serves as convincing testimony that SHE wants this more!

The next thing I realize, I find myself in the prayer prairie, on my back, tied down to the cornfield congregation, spread-eagled and mostly de-clothed, primed to consecrate some type of relationship. Either we got here via a clever scene change or she drove like hell. If the latter proves true, I best saddle up for some serious consecrating.

"Did my driving scare you, Dinky."

Ho boy! She wants this. Sheeee wants this. She... stops? And sits up?

"Dinky? You and the Russells...?"

"How kinky are you, woman?!"

"No," checking my restricting ropes. "It's just... it's just that I know you and the Russells talked. I mean... really talked for once."

Uh oh. Keep the body limp and go with the flow.

Could we all shut up and get busy here?

"I wanted to know before we..."

Get busy, baby! Say it! Say it!!!

"How can you be so tame after finding out... your best friend... is your aunt?"

Hey, buddy?! Kind of lacking blood flow down here!! Hey! No blood flow!!!

– THE END? PUH-LEEZE! –

ABOUT THE AUTHOR

 Cyrus Williams was born in Amarillo and grew up in Champaign, IL, before relocating to Knoxville in 2014. While an author, Cyrus is also is a motivational speaker, screenwriter, freelance writer and actor who loves voice-over work. In addition to recording the many voices for The Other Guy's audiobook, he also wrote and sang its soundtrack single, *My Truck Cheated on Me and My Wife Broke Down in Texas*.

Although one is more apt to find him smiling and sharing an intriguing sense of humor, his most distinctive characteristic is a boisterous laugh. Without a doubt, you know when he is near you.

Cyrus is currently pursuing an MBA from The University of Tennessee. In his free time, he most enjoys watching his wife and kids showcase their talents and creativity in music, theater, art and academia.

please also enjoy The Other Guy's soundtrack single

CYRUS WILLIAMS

MY TRUCK CHEATED ON ME
AND MY WIFE BROKE DOWN IN
TEXAS

THE
OTHER
GUY
BOOK SOUNDTRACK

available via iTunes, Amazon Music, Google Play and other e-stores

www.ingramcontent.com/pod-product-compliance
Lightning Source LLC
Chambersburg PA
CBHW050751250626
47155CB00005B/2013